SOLITAIRE

SOLITAIRE

Mojmir Drvota

Ohio State
University Press

Columbus, Ohio

Copyright © 1974
The Ohio State University Press

Cataloging in Publication Data

Drvota, Mojmir.
  Solitaire.

  I. Title.
PZ4.D7892So   [PS3554.R64]   813'.5'4   74-9557

ISBN 0-8142-0212-8

Manufactured in the United States

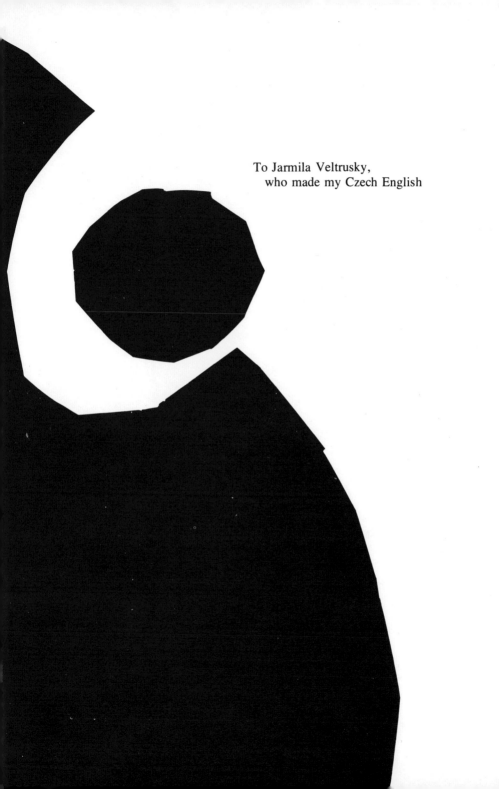

To Jarmila Veltrusky,
who made my Czech English

SOLITAIRE

PART ONE

Somebody was calling him.

Martin got up, dressed, kicked aside some odds and ends that had been left behind after his house-cleaning and went out into the night. There was a naked girl lying by the fountain in the square and pouring water out of a jar on her shoulder.

"Someone called me," Martin said to her.

"I did."

"Anything important? I was nearly asleep."

"Someone wants to see you." She put down the jar and enveloped herself in gleaming black velvet. "Come along."

Martin thought he knew the whole town, but before long he found that they were going down little streets where he had never been before.

"Who wants to see me?" Martin asked impatiently. She later laid a finger on his lips. He kissed it and was surprised by its taste.

"I taste of honey," laughed the girl. "Here we are." She pointed to the iron gate of a garden across the street.

"Go straight in. The door will be open."

Martin hestitated. "I should like . . . "

"Another kiss?"

"No. I don't really know . . . To say goodbye and thank you."

"Some other time," she said with a smile and slipped away into the darkness.

From the outside it was a very modern villa, with unexpected contours and recesses. Martin came into a vast hall, which was half shrouded in mysterious shadows. It even had a few little clouds floating in it. They were not very big, to be sure, but Martin had never seen any private clouds before.

"You are late," a bell-like voice rang out somewhere.

The light grew stronger and Martin was able to make out a man dressed in perfectly tailored evening clothes. Even the small hole on the left side of the breast would not have mattered, but it went right through the man and revealed a landscape with a range of mountains in the background. That made Martin uneasy.

His host immediately sensed Martin's feeling.

"A direct hit," he remarked. "I have to keep practicing all the time. I am sure you realize that."

"Yes," replied Martin.

"We want to send you on a certain very dangerous assignment. Two men before you have already lost their lives. We have got their ashes," the man added emphatically, as if Martin doubted him.

"Who is 'we'?" Martin stopped him.

"I beg your pardon. My name is Abel. Make sure you remember that. I represent . . . " the man waved his arm in a sweeping gesture. "You understand me?"

"Yes." Martin smiled. He had been waiting a long time for this opportunity.

"I can give you a fairly substantial sum of money for the journey, but first you will receive a set of instructions. It is a very beautifully bound book, with many exquisite illustrations. I am sure you will like it. Sit down, I shall be right back."

Martin sat down on the floor, which was made of stained and polished wood. A solemn chorale of some kind could faintly be heard through the gaps between the boards.

The host returned almost immediately.

"I cannot find it. Another time," he said with impatience.

"Don't worry about it. What is my assignment?"

"This is the address of the people concerned." He gave Martin a piece of paper. "We do not know what is going on out there. You must get in among them and find out all about it. We have the impression that it has to do with some idea or discovery. Something of that sort."

Martin glanced at the paper with the address.

"You have an absolutely free hand. We have already sent several people there; one even tried to insinuate himself among them by being born there. But so far no one has returned," the host said in a tone of regret.

"What language is the address written in?" asked Martin.

"Excuse me." The man looked at the paper. "Coptic script. Evidently it is an old address. They may have moved. They keep moving. But that is your affair. Anything else?"

"You said something about money."

The man gave him a handful of paper. It was mainly old bills of delivery, receipts, and some checks for things left at the cleaners.

"That will do to start with."

"Thank you." Martin put the scraps of paper in his pocket.

At the door, his host remembered another thing. "If you find yourself in trouble and need help, all you have to do is pick up the telephone and we shall call a meeting right away. But don't overdo it. We are a little behindhand as it is."

"I should like to thank you for everything that . . . "

The man waved it aside. "Some other time. And my best regards to your fiancée."

The door closed.

In front of the house, a black limousine was waiting for Martin.

"Home to my place," Martin ordered the chauffeur.

"No, sir. I have already received my instructions."

"Is that so?" Martin snapped angrily. "May I at least ask where we are going?"

"To your fiancée."

"You know I don't have one!" exclaimed Martin.

"That really is regrettable," said the chauffeur with a grin.

After a long, bumpy ride they stopped at the fountain in the square. Martin ran to the girl with the jar.

"Why do you claim to be my fiancée?" he burst out roughly.

"Please turn around, I am naked," she answered flirtatiously.

Martin turned his back to her.

"I am waiting for you to answer."

The trickling of water monotonously portioned out the darkness. In the distance a violin sounded, continually repeating the same few notes. Someone was learning to play.

"How did you get on?" asked the girl.

"Well. Very well. But that does not answer my question."

"Did they give you the assignment?"

Martin swung round sharply. "How do you know? Who told you?"

"Everyone knows that, surely?"

"No. That is not true! No one knows."

The girl smiled quietly.

"Why, of course, you are one of them. They sent you to fetch me. Obviously. But you ought not to talk so loudly."

"No one can hear me."

"You are a pretty girl," Martin tried another approach.

She stretched, undulating gracefully, and then said, "I ordered some music. Do you hear it?"

"Why?" he whispered.

"For the dead. I know so many of them by now that I cannot help feeling sorry for them all. One used to bring me flowers. Women like that kind of thing. Do you know why?"

"Quiet, somebody is coming."

It was a young man, who was approaching with the jerky movements of a chessman. He did not make any steps and yet kept coming nearer and nearer. The smile he wore was clearly of no recent date, indeed his whole face was, in some way, shabby, battered and so ancient that it did not look like a face at all. He was so close now that Martin had to move out of his way.

"I have come to warn you," said the young man. "Two have died already and you will be the third. The rule of three!" He disappeared in one powerful movement.

"It is them," said the girl, "the others."

"But for heaven's sake, if they already know who I am and what I am supposed to do, how can I go there among them?"

"You will have to get a disguise," said the girl without any interest. "I should just love some potato salad," she added voluptuously.

"Disguise? What disguise? Why don't you try to help me? I am desperate."

"Lie down by me for a while. Everything is always easier in the morning."

She took him in her arms. But not with love, only as a comforter, whose arms are already full though her heart is still empty. She hummed him to sleep with an old forgotten drinking song.

2

The dealer in disguises had a little shop in the basement. When Martin came in, he was stitching together the dignified exterior of a prime minister. The remnants of a general's uniform were lying about on the floor.

"I am always getting them damaged in assassinations," the dealer smiled apologetically. "What can I do for you?"

Martin looked around. "You do not seem to have a very large selection."

The dealer rose solemnly to his feet. "Our establishment is the oldest, the most reliable and the best supplied of all. Obviously you have not tried anywhere else yet and so you cannot make a fair comparison. Please come back when you have checked."

"There is no need for that, no need at all," Martin tried to soothe him. He started going through the clothes and costumes hung out on long racks.

"Be careful," warned the dealer. "Some of the disguises still have people in them, left over from when they were last used. They will be quite dry by now, so you need not feel squeamish about them. We have not had the time to clean the clothes yet. Otherwise everything is in order."

The atmosphere in the unaired room was very stuffy. Martin stopped and decided to take the costume nearest to him.

"Those are poets," came from behind him. "I see you are

very particular in your tastes, sir. Next to them you have religious fanatics. My assistant has got them a bit mixed up.''

Martin dropped his outstretched hand and began to push his way back.

The dealer laid his work aside and looked at him searchingly.

"Do you know what you want, or are you just looking for something to fit you?"

"I need a disguise, but I should like something . . . "

"Something special, if I understand, sir?"

Martin smiled wearily. "What disguise are you wearing?"

The dealer gave a start, but in a trice he was himself again.

"I am me," he said with unnecessary emphasis.

"Of course. I just wanted to make sure."

"But we shall find something for you, too," the dealer almost whispered. With a conspiratorial air he took hold of Martin and led him to a wall covered with heavy hangings. "Come with me. And be careful how you go. We have not managed to get it paved yet." He drew the ornamental material aside, revealing a thick oak door bound with wrought iron. It opened with a rending screech. The dealer stopped Martin.

"Promise you will not talk about it to anyone."

"I promise," said Martin impatiently.

"I know you will talk about it anyway. But I want to make sure, too," the dealer sighed and led Martin into a dark, narrow, underground passage. It was damp and slippery. Martin stumbled along, his feet slithering. At one point he even stepped on some big splinters of glass, which crunched under his weight.

"Once upon a time bandits used to hide out here," the dealer informed him. "But that was long ago. You need not be afraid of them now."

"Is there still far to go?" asked Martin.

"I don't know," came the answer. "I have not been here for so long that I am not even sure if we are going the right way."

Martin felt the walls on both sides and asked, "Do you mean to say we could go a different way?"

"Any way at all. It is dark everywhere, as you see, and in the dark . . . " The dealer tripped and swore. "It is ghastly in here," he said after a while. "If you knew how I hate it all." He sounded almost as if he were crying.

They went on in silence.

"There! Do you see?" The dealer stopped excitedly. A faint glow of light had appeared far ahead of them.

"Let's go," said Martin briskly.

Soon they found themselves in a large underground cave, full of light and stalactites.

"Fantastic, isn't it?" the dealer said with enthusiasm. "And all that light! These are genuine stalactites, you know." He went over to one that hung from an enormous height, almost down to the ground. "Fifty gold pieces a pound. But I am thinking of letting this one grow right down to the ground. It will be far more valuable then. What do you think of the idea?"

"Excellent."

"But it grows so slowly." The dealer patted its gleaming surface. "I really don't know if I shall live to see it."

"Of course you will. You are still a young man."

"Isn't this place fabulous?" the dealer broke out enthusiastically again. "There is so much room that you can turn somersaults. Look!" He rolled head over heels on the ground and looked at Martin with triumph.

To Martin's surprise, the ground was covered with a thick carpet patterned with a map that represented some unknown country. It showed rivers, mountain ranges, cities and towns.

"Don't you want to turn a somersault too?" said the dealer, romping about on the carpet.

"I say, what kind of a map is that?" asked Martin. "That is the country where you are going," came the unexpected answer. "A unique specimen. They have abolished all map-making on account of their enemies. Somersault?"

"No, thank you." Martin carefully examined the map. "Is it oriented to the North?"

"Why to the North?" the dealer rose and dusted his clothes.

"That is the usual way."

"Silly idea. What is in the North? Some Northern Lights, maybe, and otherwise nothing but ice and the cold. And the nights are too long. What can you sell under those circumstances? A ghost here and there, but even those will become hackneyed after a while and then people will start bringing them back and complaining they don't work properly."

"Perhaps. But that is not why we came here," said Martin, not taking his eyes off the map. "Where do you keep those disguises?"

"Oh, yes. Please wait a minute. I have to look round for them." The dealer vanished between the stalactites. The next moment, his face reappeared out of the darkness. "Please be careful not to break my stalactites. They are virulently poisonous. I shall be back shortly."

Martin knelt down, so that he could study the map in

detail. He found that it was a very ancient one. It marked some towns that no longer existed, and others, newer ones, were missing altogether. Besides, there were certain signs he did not understand. On the whole, the map looked more like an ornamental picture.

Martin crawled over on to a yellowish area, which had the words "hic sunt leones" woven into it. "This is the way I shall go in," Martin decided. He stared at the plain, monochrome area, and as he did so, he suddenly noticed a strange sign. It did not make any sense. And yet the symbol had an utterly disquieting effect. It suggested, in turn, a well, a mouth, an arabic letter, a grave, an earring, a hill, a glass and a cradle.

The dealer came back. "Are you trying to turn a somersault?"

"No," snapped Martin. "Do you happen to know what this sign means?"

"A bit of dirt off your shoe. Now I shall have to have the carpet cleaned. I am not supposed to bring anyone in here, but I always was a fool."

"You are not going to get upset about such a trifle, are you? Have you brought my disguise?"

The dealer fired up with interest. "I have just realized that you do not need a disguise at all. What you are wearing is excellent. Let me finish, please. But there is one thing you must have — a mask. A lightning change, you see, and it is only a small piece of luggage. Here! I have brought several for you to choose from. They are the best things we have in stock."

Martin examined a few of the masks, but none appealed to him particularly.

"I'll take them all," he decided.

"All?"

"Yes. How much are they?" Martin took out the money he had been given.

"I'll charge it to your account," the dealer firmly refused it.

"I did not know I had an account with you," said Martin.

"You have had one for ages. And now let us go. But you need not come back with me. There is another way out that is shorter and actually rather more comfortable. And it leads there." The dealer stabbed a finger into the air. "Or is there something else you want to do here?"

"No," answered Martin. "Show me the way."

The dealer led him to the side of the cave where a dark, narrow passage opened out. "This way."

Martin peered into the darkness.

"You cannot get lost. Keep to the right and you will be there at sunrise."

"Well, goodbye, then."

"Thank you for your visit, and please come again." The dealer gave a roguish wink. "Wouldn't you like to turn just one somersault before you go?"

Martin stepped out into the darkness.

"At your service any time," a voice called out after him, breaking against the walls of the passage.

3

The sun was at its zenith when, in the distance, Martin sighted an oasis. It was not like a fata morgana, because a carillon playing Christmas carols could be heard coming from it.

"I did take the right direction, then," whispered Martin. He had imagined at first that he would be thirsty, get sunstroke and lose his way. But as it turned out, his only difficulty was that his feet kept sinking deep into the hot sand, which made his progress rather more arduous and slow.

When he came near enough to make out separate objects, he saw that the oasis had people in it. He reached for his masks and selected the one that had the look of an amiable but weary pilgrim, craving for water. Actually, it had a sort of half-grimace around the mouth as well, but that could be interpreted in any number of ways. In the shade of a palm tree, two men in long white robes sat and conversed in loud voices. A musical clock embedded in the sand behind them had just finished the carillon and was now getting ready with a whirr to embark on some other performance. Farther on, a young girl was sweeping the dunes with a big rush broom. She was moving about with great energy and singing a song about the silvery moon — her lover.

As Martin uttered a greeting, the musical clock struck twelve. Both men looked up.

"You have come exactly on time," the first said approvingly.

"You were expecting me?" wondered Martin.

"Well, you are an amiable, weary pilgrim craving for water, aren't you?"

Before Martin could reply, the second man added: "A pilgrim who brings us a message?"

"That must be the grimace!" thought Martin. He was annoyed with the dealer for getting him into this.

"Well?"

"Yes," nodded Martin.

The men waited for a while. "What is the message, then?" the second one finally asked.

"The black dog has brought the torch — hide the pearl," said Martin. As he spoke, he poured sand from one hand to the other.

"Really?!" exclaimed the first man.

"Haven't you made a mistake?" The second man stepped right up against Martin. They stared into each other's eyes for several tense seconds. But Martin did not flinch.

"All right, go and have a drink now," the man said at last.

On his way to the well, Martin passed the girl. She was so absorbed in her work and singing that she hardly noticed him. Martin found a bottle made of ass's hide and threw it into the well. The rope to which it was attached slipped away with amazing speed, but still the skin did not hit the water. Martin bent down and looked into the well. In its dark depths glittered stars of all sizes and colors. There were many of them. After a while Martin felt the end of the rope slipping out of his hand and falling. It happened so fast that he did not even try to catch it. He gazed at the stars and felt their chill.

"My name is Azyza," a girl's provocative voice said behind him.

Martin straightened up, but the sun dazzled him so that he saw nothing but flashing wheels of color.

"It is night there," the girl laughed and then went on, "Did you bring them good news!"

"I don't know."

By the time Martin regained his sight, the girl had gone.

He went back to the two men. They were sitting in the same place and both now had long beards.

"I say it is so," the second man was saying. "Though maybe only in certain circumstances. To me, however, a void is merely an absence of being, but it is still far from being nonexistence. For nonexistence is a positive value, it is the absolute opposite of existence, you see? It is something utterly incomprehensible, it is, figuratively speaking, an explosion of impossibility. It is a shock of appalling force. And it is by this very force that it is instantly nullified and — this is the marvellous thing — it becomes the complete reverse of itself, it becomes possibility and, what is more, it becomes existence, but only once it has utterly destroyed itself. That is why, between existence and nonexistence, there is not, and cannot be, any relation whatever. Only the fact that they turn into each other without ever touching." Wearily, he stretched out on the sand.

"Hm, hm," muttered the first man, rocking back and forth. "The trouble is that you always start out with nonexistence. But how does existence turn into nonexistence?"

"I don't know," whispered his companion. Suddenly, he laughed. "Have you heard what a fool Calixenes made of himself?"

"Did he really? What happened?"

"He put a small ad in the paper — you know he has set up as a prophet — well, he put in a small ad: 'prophet seeks multitudes to lead.' And he is such a skinflint that to save paying for a second one, he added: 'also gods looking for prophets please apply.' " They burst into uproarious laughter.

"That is the absolute limit, isn't it?" gasped the second man. "Killing two birds with one stone like that. I have never heard anything like it."

Azyza passed close by them and disappeared among the trees. The men's laughter quickly died away.

"She has gone to change," whispered the first man.

"She is getting to be more and more provocative," remarked the second man, his eyes fixed on the spot where Azyza had vanished. When she reappeared, she was wearing a dress that clung tightly to her body. Round her neck she had a necklace of fisheyes, strung on a cord.

Not looking at anyone, she walked away, towards the opposite side of the oasis.

The first man got up without taking his eyes off her. But his friend quickly caught hold of him. "You can't do that. Wait! That is impossible."

He looked at Martin. "Call her! Well, go on, dammit, call her."

"Azyza!" called Martin.

She stopped and slowly turned around. Both men ran towards her. With a smile, she passed between them and came up to Martin.

"Did you want me for something?"

"Those gentlemen wanted me to call you."

"And you?"

He looked at her hips, then at her breasts. "Where did you get that necklace from?"

"A friend." She slowly raised her hands, unfastened the necklace and let it fall to the ground.

"There is something on your face," she said suddenly. Martin hastily felt his cheek. The mask was still in place.

The musical clock gave another whirr and a moment later the carillon started up again.

The girl came so close to Martin that their bodies touched. She had an acrid smell of a dampened fire.

"What message have you brought them?"

"The black dog . . ."

"Kill them," she whispered all of a sudden.

Martin shook his head.

With a snakelike wriggle, Azyza began to slip out of her clothes.

"They are watching you," whispered Martin.

She handed him a stone. Her breasts were almost bare now. Martin took the stone and threw it as hard as he could at the spot where the two men were standing. Both fell without a sound.

Martin pushed Azyza away and ran to them. He knelt down and gazed at their outflung limbs and staring eyes. Then he got up and walked back to Azyza.

"Well, now I must go and make dinner," she said in a matter-of-fact tone, modestly adjusting her dress.

"I won't have anything to eat," said Martin.

"Of course not. Do you know what you have to do now?"

"Yes," answered Martin hesitantly.

"I'll come with you." She fastened her necklace, then she

took Martin by the hand and led him to the well. Martin sat down on the edge and glanced at Azyza. She caressed him and said in a doleful voice, "I don't know what I shall do all alone here." But then she laughed at herself. "Someone else is bound to turn up. Well, what are you waiting for?"

"Head first," said Martin. He crouched down, leaped up and the next moment he was sprinting away into the desert as fast as he could go.

"You hideous beast! You coward! You monster, you villain! You ought to be ashamed of yourself, you damned scoundrel!" Azyza screamed after him.

Martin kept on running as fast as ever.

"Murderer! Assassin! He has killed two people! Catch him! Murder! Police!"

By this time both Azyza and the carillon were almost out of hearing.

4

Martin had been running at full speed for many hours. The scrub-covered steppe seemed to be rolling backwards under his feet of its own accord. Round his ears, a gentle breeze fluttered, stirred up by his own motion. It was very pleasant. Toward evening, when the sun grew less scorching, it occurred to him that he ought to think about taking some rest.

"I can't see myself ever coming to a stop at all," Martin said. He often talked to himself nowadays. "This second wind is a marvellous thing."

Night was falling and the sky was full of stars. "I have got my bearings," Martin said to himself. He headed for the pole star and ran on.

A crescent moon came out and three stars appeared in its bow. "I saw a flag like that once, but now I cannot remember what country it belonged to." Martin went on chatting to himself. "It is funny to see a sign in the sky. I thought all symbols were made up by people."

"Would you mind if I joined you?" said a voice close beside him.

"Please do," Martin replied. "But I don't stop anywhere."

"That's all right. I just don't want to run alone," the voice continued.

"Who are you?" asked Martin. He remembered his stock of masks, but it was too late now. And anyway, it was practically impossible to see anything.

"I am about forty years old," the man answered. "I have a knapsack on my back, and I shall be glad to have this stretch of country behind me. It is a dangerous region. Robbers, you know."

"I didn't know."

They ran on side by side for some time.

"Are you a robber?" asked Martin.

The man ran so lightly that it was impossible to tell whether he was still by Martin's side.

"I am a ghost," replied the voice after a while.

"Nonsense," snapped Martin.

The ground no longer gave off the heat it had absorbed during the day. It grew distinctly colder.

"Nonsense," repeated Martin. He glanced sideways, but there was nothing to see.

"You will lose your direction. Keep your eyes on the star," said the ghost.

"Are you a jinni?" Martin tried a different approach.

"No. I don't work in bottles. I could not stand it."

"If you are a ghost, how come you are running?"

"I am not running," came the answer. "And I am not flying. I simply am, you understand?"

"Does that mean that you are everywhere?"

"What business is it of yours how I do it?" the ghost flared up. "Why the devil shouldn't I run, too, if I feel like it?"

There was a crash of thunder, but no lightning appeared. Martin did not answer.

"Are you angry?" the voice said coaxingly after a while.

"I should like to be alone again," said Martin.

"That is impossible. Because of the robbers, you know?"

"Are you afraid?" Martin asked scornfully.

"Of course I am. I am afraid for you."

"So you are my guardian spirit, are you?"

"Look, that is something you don't understand. You would start asking where I was when you broke your arm, what I was doing that time they accused you of stealing the typewriter and so on and so forth. My nerves won't stand all that explaining, let alone trying to make it sound logical. Anyway, why should I bother?"

Suddenly, a shot rang through the night.

"There, what did I tell you? They are shooting," the ghost exclaimed.

The shot had obviously been fired very far away, so the bullet could not be heard. For a split second, Martin thought it was a clap of thunder.

"Was that someone shooting at me?" asked Martin. There was something about it that did not jibe. He felt for one of his masks and put it on. It was the face of someone who has traveled long and purposefully, a man determined to overcome the fatigue of his journey by exacting the conditions in which he is accustomed to live. And by being ready to divert himself with the sight of new places.

"It sounded like a shot at someone on the run," said the ghost after a brief pause. "But it wounds me."

"Physically?" Martin twitted him.

"Spiritually," snapped the ghost.

"Are they going to go on shooting?"

"I don't know. I am not a clairvoyant. Do you think that mask is going to do you any good?"

Martin touched his face. Then he reached out to his side. There was nothing there.

"I say, where exactly are you running to?" asked the ghost.

"I'm following the star. To the North."

"You will have to bear slightly to one side in order to get to the port. Otherwise you will end up on a deserted, rocky shore."

"What are you talking about? What shore?"

"Look out!" roared the ghost, but it was too late. Martin fell as if his feet had been cut from under him. The world still seemed to be running past him, but it was clear that that was only an illusion.

"What happened?" whispered Martin. Sharp edges of some kind were cutting painfully into his body.

"You stopped too abruptly," said the ghost.

"I feel as if I were still floating," complained Martin.

"Open your eyes," the voice advised him.

Martin tried to do so, for an instant he glimpsed a piece of the night sky, but his eyelids immediately closed again.

"The day is beginning to dawn," the voice pointed out. "I'll have to hurry."

"You are not going to leave me here like this, are you?" Martin flared up. "In the middle of this wilderness?"

"Yes I am," answered the voice. "It is not far to the shore now. When you feel a bit better, you will go on with your journey. If you cannot manage any other way, crawl on all fours. Goodbye."

"Go to the devil," Martin shouted after him.

After a while, he made another attempt to feel the object that was pressing into him. It was a big wooden wheel, half buried in the ground; the spokes were skillfully carved in the shape of human figures.

Martin turned over to the other side. Less than a yard away from him, a sheer precipice dropped down to a little town that nestled at its foot, and beyond that stretched the sea. From the cliff where Martin lay, the whole thing looked like an expensive toy. The streets of the town were empty, a few boats bobbed up and down beside the jetty. A fresh morning breeze was blowing.

"Are you dead, sir?" inquired a voice at Martin's back. He swung around sharply, instinctively on the defensive. Before him there stood an elderly, gaunt little fellow in uniform, with a lantern hanging on his chest.

"No," said Martin. He tried to get up, but flopped helplessly back on the ground. He sat there, his body swaying to and fro.

"Are you a suicide, sir?" the little man asked again. "We get those from time to time, but hardly anyone knows how to go about it properly. Usually they catch on the scrub and just get a few bruises. A lot of box grows around here."

"I am not a suicide. Who are you?"

"A conductor, sir. Years ago a stagecoach used to come this way, but then something went wrong with it, so now I am left here alone."

"Can you get me down to the town? I have been running all night," Martin added emphatically.

"You do look exhausted, sir," acknowledged the conductor. "The shortest way to town from here is a kind of goat track along which our mule maintains communication. It is a very reliable animal, sir, and capable of bearing quite a load. His name is Alex."

"Could he carry me?"

"He certainly could. Did you want to catch the boat, sir?"

"The boat? Yes — that is an excellent idea. When does it sail?"

"At noon today. If there is any wind. If there is wind

earlier, it will leave earlier. And if there is no wind at noon . . . ''

"Where is that mule?"

"I don't know, sir. But in any case there is no station here. You must go to the station — I have to keep order here, otherwise our whole system of transport would break down."

Martin got up. "All right, take me to the station."

"Are you going to leave that wheel there, sir?"

"It is not mine. Let's go."

"It might come in handy. It is a beautiful piece of carving." The conductor bent down. "It was brightly colored, originally. You see, it still has traces of paint on it."

"I am in a hurry, conductor," said Martin emphatically.

"Unfortunately, the mule does not leave for another two hours, sir," replied the conductor.

Martin made a threatening step towards him: "I am leaving right now. Get the mule ready."

"Nonsense, sir. I cannot have you messing up my timetable. Besides, where do you see a mule? Look around, sir — is there a mule anywhere about? What would a mule be doing in this wilderness?" The conductor extinguished the lamp on his chest. "We must economize — there is enough light now."

"Show me the track."

"I can do that, sir." The conductor licked a finger and raised it into the air. "The wind is rising," he announced. "You haven't got a hope of catching the boat."

"Show me the track," yelled Martin.

"Gladly, sir. Come with me."

They walked along the edge of the cliff. The light kept growing stronger. The sky in the East began to turn pink.

"I don't see any track," said Martin.

"Nor do I, sir. And I am older than you. After all, it is only a very narrow track, little used. It is so faint, that some people say it is not a track at all. Even local people say so. I bet you will not recognize it even when we are standing right by it."

Martin peered over the edge of the cliff. Its face was somewhat more gradual there, no longer a straight drop. "Is it here?" he asked.

The guard came up to him and carefully glanced down. "There, you see, now I am not quite sure myself. — No, I don't think it is here."

Martin grabbed him by the collar and bent him over the edge. The conductor gave a shriek of fear.

"You are laying hands on an official person, sir. There are laws about that."

"Is it here?" Martin repeated angrily.

"I suffer from dizziness, sir. If anything happens to me, you will be in real trouble."

Martin was shaking the conductor violently to and fro. "Let me go, sir. I cannot recognize anything like this, can I?"

Martin relaxed his grip.

"I have never seen the track," gabbled the conductor. "The mule knows about it, but I don't. I always sit on him, shut my eyes and let him carry me down. I have to keep imagining that I am riding over level ground, otherwise I could not endure it."

The conductor was now standing with his back to the cliff edge, and Martin a step in front of him, crimson with rage. Once more he raised his hand at the conductor.

"I will try, sir," screamed the conductor. "I'll try to see if it is here. Give me just a second to nerve myself."

The conductor spun around, turning his back to Martin, stretched out his arms and suddenly jumped. Martin dashed to the edge, but it was too late to catch him.

The conductor fell onto a ledge on the cliff face, ran a few steps, fell, rolled over and over for a while, got up, fell down again, turned a few somersaults backwards, caught in the scrub for a moment, rose to his feet, made a few jumps and disappeared from Martin's sight.

"Conductor!" yelled Martin. "Conductor!"

Some loosened earth and pebbles rolled down the slope; now and then something in the scrub crackled.

"Conductor!"

The sounds on the slope faded away in the distance.

"I must go after him," Martin swiftly decided. He dropped his legs over the edge, then his trunk, pushed himself off a little and began to slide down. He went faster and faster. His course was full of bumps, unexpected jumps, extraordinary twists of the body, leaps, tumbles, slips, momentary holds.

At last Martin landed at the foot of the cliff. He lay there, panting for breath. His cuts and scratches began to ooze blood.

"The boat!" flashed through Martin's head, but he collapsed as soon as he tried to get up.

5

Martin opened his eyes and saw a banner with the word
"Welcome" written on it. It was strung between the last two
houses of a short little street leading to the foot of the cliff.
The inscription was written in an unskilled hand; the big
black letters leaned in all directions, the thickness of the
individual strokes varied, the spaces between them were
uneven. In spite of everything, the banner as a whole had an
air of vigor and self-confidence about it.

Martin got to his feet and tried to brush himself down, but
every movement gave him considerable pain. Moreover, he
discovered that he had lost his right shoe.

"The boat!" Martin suddenly remembered and set off at a
run for the port. By a dilapidated wharf, a broad-beamed ship
lay rocking gently. Martin ran over the gangplank and
jumped on board. The next moment the ship pulled away
from the shore; in full sail, it rode out onto the high seas.
Martin ran all round the deck but did not find anybody.
Seeing a steep companionway, he climbed down to the lower
deck. The cabin doors were shut, but one finally gave way as
he charged against it. Martin fell into a small cabin. It was
empty. He glanced back at the door and saw it had a card with
his name on it. Quite overcome, he stretched out on the berth.

It was a richly carved bed with a canopy borne up by four
gilt fauns. The rest of the furniture, however, was totally at
odds with this piece. An old oak table, its top gashed all over,

a rather bald plush armchair standing on no more than three legs, a battered cupboard painted brown and with only half a door, a hooped tub with a piece of rope for a handle, a phonograph with a horn on a sturdy chest in the corner and, on the ceiling, a lamp in a wire basket. On another chair by the table lay some carefully folded clothes and linen.

Martin felt his cheek. The mask was not there. He put a hand in his pocket and pulled out another one at random. With a few touches he fixed it on his face. He looked at the walls but did not see any mirror.

"What are you doing here?" suddenly thundered through the cabin. In the door there stood an enormous man, with an enormous beard bordering his stern face. Some little bells hanging round his neck effectively softened his rough appearance. Martin sprang up from the bed.

"Are you the captain?" he asked.

The man thought it over. "Yes," he said finally.

"I am a passenger on your ship, captain," said Martin.

"My name is on the door."

The man glanced at the door, tore the card off and threw it on the floor.

"Let us pray," he then commanded in a peremptory voice.

"I have no mirror here, captain," announced Martin. "And I have lost a shoe somewhere."

The captain knelt down in the doorway and began to jingle his little bells.

Martin copied him. "What am I to jingle with?"

The captain threw him a few bells. "When we finish praying," he said softly, "I shall throw you out."

They jingled on.

"Let us go!" ordered the captain at last.

"I should be glad to pay for a ticket," Martin explained, but he received no answer. "Or I could work my passage." The captain stopped and gave Martin a searching look. "Come along," he said after some reflection. They climbed down the steep companionway. On the lowest deck, the captain took a big key and opened the heavy door of the storeroom. Here, in a long net, lay a heaving jumble of bodies covered with moist slime. Large fish and half-naked human bodies were slithering aimlessly over one another.

"Some of them have already died," said the captain and handed Martin a small green watering can. "You will water them three times a day. In the morning, at noon, and in the evening."

"Yes, sir."

"The key will hang on this nail here."

"I have only one shoe, captain," Martin tried once more.

The captain shut the door and started back up the companionway. Somewhere in the hold of the ship a bell sounded.

"Can you sing?" he asked, turning to Martin.

"Only a little. I have something of a musical ear, but my voice is untrained."

The captain shrugged.

"Those down below are prisoners?" Martin ventured to ask.

The captain gave a peculiar smile. They went into the dining room on the first deck. It was a very long but narrow room. Down the center ran a table, carefully laid with plates, knives, and forks. The captain took a seat at the far end and picked up his knife and fork. Martin remained standing by the wall. They waited. The ship rolled from side to side.

"It looks as if there won't be anything today," muttered

the captain after a long while. He laid down his knife and fork and walked out. Martin picked up one of the plates and turned it over. It was branded with some words in a language he did not know and a sketch of a medieval town. Somewhere upstairs some dance music struck up. Martin put the plate down and set out in search of the sound.

On the deck, two couples were dancing a lithe tango. They danced with such concentration that they did not even notice Martin. The long, elastic movements of the dancers did not correspond to the rhythm of the music. By the main mast, a man of waxy pallor stood beating time with a stick of candy. Martin approached him. But the man stared past, his eyes fixed on the faint outline of the coast disappearing in the remote distance.

"We seem to be going very fast," Martin said to him. But the man was clearly oblivious of his existence.

"I hope the wind will hold," Martin tried once again.

At that moment one of the dancing couples sprang over the handrail in one gliding leap and vanished over the side of the ship.

"Man overboard!" yelled Martin.

The conductor laid his baton carefully on the deck floor and began to applaud. Martin dashed to the rail and leaned out over it. The lost couple went on dancing without a pause over the surface of the sea in the rhythm of the waves. The dancers' feet barely skimmed the water. In sweeping curves they moved away, wholly absorbed in their dance.

Martin turned round when the applause behind his back stopped. The conductor was no longer on the deck. The second couple carried on with their dance, which was growing ever more aggressive. With each step the man wedged himself further and further into his partner, so that at times it seemed as if it were only one body that was dancing. They merged more and more completely. As they flashed past Martin, tears suddenly gushed from the man's eyes.

Martin turned away and slowly walked to the steps leading down below.

In his cabin, Martin found a printed program for the day. Among other things, it said that the watering of the storeroom was being postponed until further notice. The position, direction, and speed of the ship were given in strange units. The heading concerning the weather and the state of the sea was crossed out and over it, written in red ink, was the announcement: "Urgent! The dancing competition on deck is canceled as of tomorrow. Instead, there will be emergency drill (fire, hurricane, hole in the keel). Attendance compulsory for all. Low entrance fee. Weather permitting, there will be mutiny practice."

Martin put the program down and began to walk round the cabin. In passing, he opened the chest and discovered that it was full of gold coins, long withdrawn from circulation. He picked up a handful and let them fall back. They rang as in days gone by. He turned to the phonograph, wound it up and put on a record. It was an ancient dirge. Martin lay down on the bed and closed his eyes. He saw two wooden angels floating on streams of blue air. But there was not enough room for them in the cabin. They kept bumping into the walls and against each other. It occurred to Martin that he should open the porthole for them, but he could not summon the strength to get up.

The panic ringing of a bell woke Martin. It was morning. He jumped off the bed and ran up on deck. The captain was standing there with a whistle in his mouth. Martin sprang to attention. The captain rolled a barrel that was standing at his feet toward the opening to the lower decks, poured its contents into the hold of the ship, struck a match and threw it onto the liquid. It burst into flames with a violent bang.

"Ready!" bellowed the captain and started blowing his whistle.

Martin snatched up a container of some sort and ran about looking for water.

"Where is the water?" he called out to the captain as he dashed past.

"You can just pretend," answered the captain.

So Martin swung his container to and fro over the flames as if he were putting them out. But the fire went on spreading with loud cracks.

"Lower the lifeboats!" ordered the captain.

Martin spun the handles on both sides of the ship. The boats hit the water. In the same instant the sails billowed out as a burst of wind thudded into them.

"Hurricane!" roared the captain. "Cut down the main mast!"

Martin wrenched an axe out of its holder and began to hack at the sturdy foot of the mast. The wind was tossing the ship in all directions. The deck rose and fell at dizzying angles.

"Faster!" urged the captain.

Martin hacked away with the axe, slipped, clambered back and again slashed out with all his might. At last the mast gave way and toppled over the side of the ship, covering the deck with a tangle of sails.

"The ship is leaking!" cried the captain.

Martin crawled out from under the sails.

"Man the pumps!" came the order.

"Where are they?" yelled Martin.

"I don't know," said the captain softly. "We may not have any."

The deck was slowly sinking to water level. The bell insistently continued ringing the alarm.

"Find a pole and pretend you are pumping," ordered the captain. "Quickly!"

Martin picked up a piece of broken spar and began pumping.

"Faster!" barked the captain.

The ship was sinking rapidly. Almost imperceptibly, its hold was growing heavier and heavier.

Suddenly the bell fell silent.

"The ship is lost!" cried the captain. "It's every man for himself!"

Upon these words he bent forward, sprang up, and vaulted in a high arc into the sea.

With feverish effort Martin collected some planks, lashed their ends to two empty barrels, threw into a sack everything he could lay his hands on, the axe, a piece of sail, a rope, an old sweater, a skin of drinking water, some grease-soaked rags, an iron hook, and a rusty lantern. Then he tied up the bag and sat down on his improvised craft. The ship sank beneath him into the depths of the sea. It occurred to him that he had better lash himself to his raft, but the next moment he fainted from exhaustion.

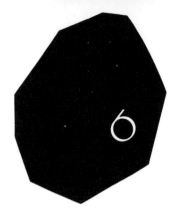

6

Martin woke up on the shore of a becalmed sea, near a dazzling white house. His raft had vanished. He got up and made for the house, meaning to rest there for a short while. He found that it was owned by a lens-polisher, who gave Martin a very friendly welcome, almost forcing the hospitality of his spacious residence upon him. The house was built around a central courtyard, with all the rooms opening on to it. Some trees and bushes grew there, all carefully tended and laid out with an extraordinarily subtle sense of shape and color. In the center there stood a triangular prism — the work of the lens-polisher. As Martin learned, however, it was not a real prism, but the statue of a prism that, it seemed, had once existed somewhere. Martin spend most of his time here, on a bench set among sweet-smelling bushes. The house was filled to overflowing with children of all shapes and sizes; all wore spectacles with frames of sumptuous forms and colors. The children were continually streaming through all the rooms and corridors in pursuit of their various amusements. Some of them knew each other only very slightly, quite often through no more than chance encounters. As a paying guest, Martin ate in the first shift, with the lens-polisher and his wife, who was, however, quite indistinguishable from her eldest daughters. For sleep, Martin was put on the fourth night shift. Everyone naturally took him for a brother who had so far kept to some other part of the house. The polisher himself recognized Martin only because his guest was not wearing spectacles yet. Martin had presented himself here in the mask of an unobtrusive guest and it gave him a rather clownish expression. He lived in constant fear that the polisher would force one of his products upon him.

"Come to my workshop," the polisher said to him after lunch on the following day. "I have something there that might interest you."

They went into a ground-floor room, from which the polisher first removed five or six children, then locked the door, and finally shut the window as well. He sat down at his worktable and Martin opposite him.

"By the way, have you ever seen so many children?"

"No," answered Martin after a short hesitation.

"Some of them look as strange to me as a postage stamp from Madagascar," said the polisher meditatively. "But that only happens sometimes and only for a moment. Then right away I recognize the familiar features and the strangeness disappears. Only I am afraid of losing my memory."

Martin shifted in his seat and gave a little cough.

"But now to come to the point," the polisher began. "Do you know which human faculty is the most important?"

"The memory?" Martin suggested tentatively.

The polisher burst out laughing. "The eye, my friend. The eye. Without the eye, there is no memory and absolutely nothing outside you. Without his eyes, man is left to himself, he remains shut up within himself. That is why I became a lens-polisher."

He picked up some pieces of glass. "You see, I make convex and concave lenses, simple as well as composite ones, which I cement together with Canadian balsam. I give people sight."

"A beautiful profession," remarked Martin.

"A profession like any other, but I have the right attitude toward it. But that is not the point. All the lenses here are ordinary ones. Do you know what I mean by that?"

"No. I have forgotten all I ever knew about the theory of optics."

The polisher waved it aside. "That doesn't matter. There is nothing interesting in it, anyway. Just ordinary optics. But now pay attention! What if there were a lens that would enable you to see right through things, that would lay them quite bare and, what is more, allow you to look beyond them?"

"That would be absolutely revolutionary. But is it possible?" interrupted Martin.

"Excuse me." The polisher went to the window, behind which several children's heads had appeared, and motioned them away. The children immediately scattered.

"What do you think this is?" The polisher laid a glass ball in front of Martin.

"A glass ball," said Martin.

"It is a combination of lenses," the polisher corrected him. "The fortuneteller's crystal ball that people later made so much fun of. Well, isn't it amusing? What do you say?"

Martin got up.

"Don't you want to take a look?"

"No."

The polisher laughed. "You mean you don't want to look through things?"

"No." Martin backed to the door. "Have you looked at me, too?"

"Of course."

"And what did you see?" Martin was ready to pounce at

the polisher's throat. The polisher was gasping with laughter. He pointed to the window. A crowd of children's faces was pressed up against it.

"What did you see?" Martin repeated with an effort.

"Nothing," exploded the polisher triumphantly. "Vision that goes through absolutely everything obviously cannot reveal anything but — nothing!"

Martin's legs gave way under him. He sat down. "Of course. That is absolutely logical," he laughed convulsively. "I say, I should love to buy that lens from you."

"It is not for sale," said the polisher, wiping away tears of laughter. "Let us leave now, and forget what you have seen. Would you like to look at our year-before-last twins?"

Martin quietly left his bed and felt his way in the dark to the door. The more slowly he opened it, the louder it creaked. In the corridor, there was a little light from the adjacent rooms. Martin slipped into the polisher's workshop and locked the door behind him. He looked around. The moon lit the room with a few streaks of blue light. But the glass ball was not where he had last seen it. Softly he began to open the cabinets filled with the polisher's tools and products. All at once, he felt he was being watched. He whirled around. By the dark wall near the door, many pairs of eyes gleamed dolefully, all bulging with horror.

"I forgot something here," Martin tried to explain.

Nobody answered.

"I do not like your looking at me like that. I hope you do not suspect . . ."

The moon disappeared behind a cloud, plunging the workshop in darkness.

"Call your father," Martin said into the black void. "I demand that you call your father," he repeated insistently after a moment.

There was absolute silence.

Martin felt for a stool and sat down on it. "I am your guest," he laughed suddenly, "You cannot do anything to me. Do you hear?"

He took a cigarette out of his pocket and put it in his mouth. Then he struck a match and held it out at arm's length. On the wall, attached to velvet pads, there lay a number of artificial eyes, spectral little balls of glass. Martin stared at them as if he could not understand. Someone tried the handle.

"Is anybody there?" asked a voice. It was the polisher.

The match went out. Martin felt his way to the window, but he bumped into several objects on the way.

"Who is there?" The polisher was banging on the door.

Martin opened the window and jumped out. The beach was in total darkness and there was nobody to be heard. He broke into a run, his hands stretched out before him. In the house behind, one window after another began to light up and a hum of human voices grew louder and louder.

"Just like stirring up an ants' nest," Martin thought. Then he vanished in the dark avenue.

7

Martin woke up in a small meadow enclosed on three sides by a forest. Along one edge there ran a deeply rutted carttrack. A stream, concealed between young saplings, bubbled on the other side. The grass and the forest were fragrant with sun, water, and resin. A vista opened out on to a landscape of undulating knolls and hills. In the distance, a village lay half-hidden but betraying its presence by a greenish church steeple.

After his night escape, Martin had slept here through the whole morning. Now he was hungry. He wandered into the forest and picked some cranberries and blueberries, which he washed down with cold water from the stream. Then he made himself a comfortable bed of moss in the shade of the trees. He lay down and half closed his eyes. A few flies hovered round him in wavering circles. High above the treetops, a bird sang.

"I can stay here another night," thought Martin. "There are heaps of mushrooms growing around here — I shan't be hungry." When he opened his eyes again, a strange man was standing before him. He looked like a pilgrim, but somehow too much so — more like a pilgrim on the stage. He was dressed in sackcloth, a staff in his hand and most of his face overgrown with a long beard. Martin gave a jump, half out of respect, half in self-defense.

"Good day," he said uncertainly.

The man nodded.

"I have been resting here a little," Martin tried to start up a conversation.

Again the man only nodded.

"I hope that is allowed."

The man nodded.

Martin felt very uncomfortable. The masks were lying close by him, but it was out of the question to use one now. "I picked a few blueberries and cranberries. Is that allowed?"

Still the man went on steadily gazing at Martin, not taking his eyes off him for a second. Now, instead of answering, the eccentric motioned Martin to get up. Then he turned and went into the forest. Martin followed, keeping a considerable distance between the man and himself. He glanced ruefully at the little heap of masks he had left lying in the moss, but he dared not go back for them.

They went on for a long time through the tall fir forest, here and there crossing a faintly trodden path. At last they came to a clearing, which had several peculiar-looking structures standing in it. Some of them were giving off smoke.

"What is it?" breathed Martin.

"Charcoal piles," replied the man. Then he led Martin into a cottage no bigger than the biggest pile. It was built of stones and earth. Martin bent his head as he went in and it took him a while to get used to the dusk in the tiny room. First he made out an open fireplace, then a roughly hewn bench and table, a small platform on the floor made of moss, grass, and leaves and covered with fur. Finally, shelves with a few pots and pans and a little open hole in the wall, serving as a window.

"Are you a charcoal burner?" asked Martin.

The man nodded. He made Martin sit down at the table and took an iron pot off the hook above the fire. He set it before Martin, together with a wooden spoon.

"Thank you." Martin cautiously scooped up a small mouthful, but to his surprise the food was delicious. The collier sat down on the bench and seemed to forget Martin's presence.

"You have beautiful country round here," said Martin when he had eaten his fill.

Without a word, the man left the hut. He began to examine one of the dome-shaped piles nearby, which had split open in a wide crack. Smoke was escaping through it.

"Thank you once again," Martin said hesitantly, "but I don't want to take up your time. You have been very kind." The collier went over to a stockade made of tree trunks lashed together with bast. A huge animal resembling an aurochs but with two strong, sharp horns, was charging about inside it. It kept butting against the stockade with a force that made it grunt.

The collier began to throw it some fodder.

"Well, I'll be going now," said Martin hesitantly.

"Goodbye."

When he had gone a few steps, he was stopped by the collier's voice: "Message."

"You think I have a message for you?" asked Martin.

The collier slowly shook his head.

"Well, do you have a message for me?"

Again the man mutely denied it.

"Someone else has a message for me?"

The collier nodded. It was clear that from now on he had lost all interest in the matter.

"When will he come?"

The collier shrugged his shoulders. He was totally engrossed in the animal inside the stockade. So Martin returned to the collier's hut. He sat down on the ground by the door and leaned against the wall of the cabin. The sun was setting.

Early the next morning, Martin was woken by the approaching sound of horse's hoofs. Soon a man dressed in a colorful, gold-embroidered suit of clothes rode into the clearing and pulled up. He took off his plumed hat to Martin.

"Her Majesty wishes to see you at once. Get ready for the journey."

"I am ready," replied Martin sleepily.

"The carriage will be here in a moment," said the messenger. Then he walked round the clearing and peered into the cabin; the collier came out towards him.

"It is dull here," he remarked to Martin. "Collier, I want to see a fight."

The collier bowed and walked away.

"What is going to happen?" asked Martin.

Before the messenger could reply, the aurochs rushed out into the clearing; it looked about and pawed the ground with its hoof.

"Not at me, stupid," the messenger said to it. "There is the collier, over there."

The animal turned its head and immediately charged against the collier, who was coming back from the stockade. It was a very cruel battle. The collier, fighting with his bare hands, was too slow for the animal. He seemed to be trying to blind it by punching it in the eye. The aurochs was too heavy, so that it could not manoeuvre easily. It always attacked in a straight line, trying to spear its opponent and slit him open with a jerk of its horn. Then the animal managed to plunge one of its horns into the collier's thigh, but he contrived to grab it by the other horn and by brute force prevent it from jerking it up. For a moment they remained locked together. The messenger clapped, tense with excitement. Little by little the collier worked his pierced leg free, but before he could turn his advantage to account, the aurochs sprang away out of his grip. Once more they stood facing each other.

"Brave, bravo," the messenger called to them.

Martin jumped at him. "I'll kill you!"

The messenger's face froze with amazement. "For heaven's sake!" he said at last. "Have I done anything to you?"

Martin took in every quiver on the messenger's face. Then he closed his eyes as if all his strength had left him.

"Look! There! Look! Aren't they fantastic?" the messenger was exclaiming, once more absorbed in the fight.

Now the collier managed to catch the aurochs by both horns and force its neck down. The animal was dragging him to and fro all over the clearing, but it could not shake him off.

A carriage glittering with magnificent gold ornaments and drawn by three pairs of milk-white horses drove into the clearing. The messenger was standing on tiptoe in the height of excitement. The aurochs had now stopped and the collier was gradually wrenching his head to one side. The animal braced itself on its hind legs in an effort to escape. But the collier did not let up.

The driver of the carriage gave a blast on a small silver trumpet.

"Right away, right away," the messenger put him off.

By now the head of the aurochs, giving under the collier's pressure, was twisted at a quite unnatural angle to the body. Suddenly something snapped and the animal's enormous body slowly turned over and fell on its side; it shuddered spasmodically and quivered all the time.

"Brave, bravo!"

The collier got up, but before he finished his second step, he collapsed with exhaustion. Blood was pouring from the wound in his leg.

"Bravo, collier! Excellent! Here!" The messenger threw some gold coins on the ground and turned to Martin. "We can go."

"But what about him? Don't you think we should help him? In a moment he will have bled to death."

The messenger laughed. "The collier? Don't be silly. In a moment he will have forgotten all about it. But now let us hurry, please. Her Grace is waiting."

The silver trumpet gave a loud metallic blast.

"It is extremely interesting," said the messenger thoughtfully as he took his seat in the carriage, "that this time they did not knock down a single charcoal pile. No one will believe me. How very, very interesting . . . "

The carriage drove out of the clearing.

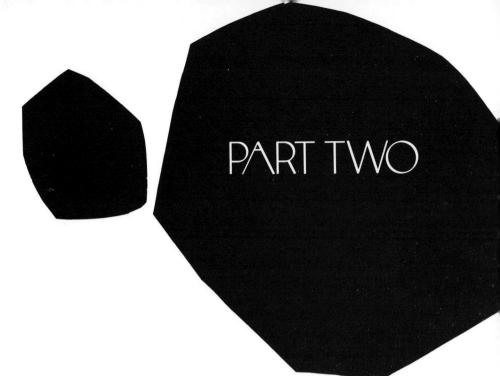

PART TWO

8

Servants led Martin into the hall of the Third Law. It was an immense underground room, with large colored stains and pictures of various parts of the human body painted in many different styles on the walls. Office desks were scattered at irregular intervals about the floor, and at each one there was an official and a group of waiting people. Martin was taken to an official surrounded by samples of different colors. The official looked up. "Where are you from?"

"I was told that Her Grace is expecting me. I do not understand why I am here," protested Martin.

"You must realize that you have to be brought before Her Grace in proper dress and also that Her Grace must know whom she is dealing with. Well?"

Martin named his country.

"Thank you. And now we shall take a look at your hair." The official peered at a color scale on the wall and checked Martin's hair against it. "You are slightly fairer and have rather more burnt sienna." The official called an assistant and ordered him to tint Martin's hair. "Let me explain — this is the correct average color for your country. We have to adjust yours in accordance with it. On the other hand, we shall take your color and modify our sample in the ratio of one to the number of inhabitants of your country. That will make our sample absolutely right again. Ingenious, isn't it?" he added with a smile.

"Now go to the next table," said the official, when Martin's hair had assumed the correct shade. "There they will check your height and weight."

Martin turned out to be a quarter of an inch shorter than the prescribed average. He was laid on a rack beside the official's table and an assistant slowly began to stretch him.

"You must excuse the discomfort we are causing you," apologized the official. "But after all, it is not our fault: you are a quarter of an inch too short, you see?"

"I see," Martin hissed with pain.

"It is generally a very quick and almost painless operation."

"I am afraid I shall faint," gasped Martin.

"That does not matter. Would you care for some refreshments?"

"No."

The official was carefully watching the gauges on the rack. "It will be over in another moment."

"Couldn't I be put to sleep?" was wrung from Martin.

"Unfortunately not. You see, we do this absolutely free and at the same time it is an adjustment that will last you for the rest of your life. You are lucky that your weight meets the requirements."

Martin did not answer because he had lost consciousness. When he came to, he was a quarter of an inch taller and seated opposite another official, who was studying his face with professional interest.

"What do you measure?" Martin asked him.

"Intelligence," replied the official and pushed several colored wooden blocks and sheets of paper covered with psychological tests in front of Martin. He picked up a stopwatch. "When I say 'Now,' start on question number one. When the bell rings, stop, wherever you have got to."

"Excuse me, but I should like to know how many more places I have to go through."

"You have hardly started. As I see, all you have had done so far is your hair, your height, and your weight. I doubt that you will get through everything today."

"The messenger told me that Her Grace wishes to see me at once," objected Martin.

"You can see that we are working as fast as possible, can't you? I should not be surprised if we stayed overtime today."

"Excuse me for interrupting once more, but in case my intelligence has to be regulated either up or down, I should like to know how you go about it."

The official smiled. "We have excellent substances that we administer by injection. The results are absolutely accurate. And not only here in my department of intelligence, but also next door in sensititivy, in will, perception, memory, and so on. You have nothing to be afraid of."

"Thank you."

"You are welcome. And now we shall begin with test number one. Get ready."

Some hours later Martin had the entire hall of the Third Law behind him. He was somewhat changed, both physically and mentally. His body hurt not only on account of the rack but also of the many injections and a whole series of minor adjustments that he had been obliged to undergo. Servants gently led him out into the fresh air.

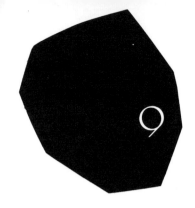

9

The hall of the Second Law occupied the whole of a large building topped with a vaulted dome. Inside, it was almost completely dark. Only some artificial stars gently drifting across the dome gave a little dim, cold light. A series of peculiar tables were slowly moving over the floor along irregular courses but never colliding.

Martin sat down in an armchair opposite a man who was just buttoning up a long black robe adorned with stars and the signs of the zodiac.

"How do you feel after being in the hands of those butchers?" he said gaily to Martin.

"I hurt all over," answered Martin. He looked around, and it seemed to him that he was moving, though he had no sense of motion. The speed appeared to be changing all the time.

"You will feel better here with us. I have been chosen to be your astrologer," explained the man.

"How do you do?"

"How do you do? This is an interesting place, isn't it?" said the astrologer, observing Martin's look.

"Immensely," replied Martin. "What do you study here?"

"Your fate."

Martin looked at the astrologer. "My fate?"

"Fates in general. Destiny. Whatever you want to call it."

"The past, the present and the future?" Martin asked cautiously.

"My dear fellow, it is absurd to study the past, because that is known. The same goes for the present. The future you will more or less shape yourself, but within the framework of certain possibilities. And it is these possibilities we are concerned with. Of course, you can also regard them as limitations that have been predestined for you. And these limitations, or if you like these possibilities, are determined by astral relations, by the constellations of the stars. Is that clear?"

"I think I understand, but you must be patient with me. They have lowered my intelligence a bit."

"That doesn't matter. Any idiot could understand what I am telling you."

At the far end of the vault there appeared a comet with a long tail that was burning up fast.

"Do you see it?" whispered the astrologer excitedly. "That one upset the fate of nearly the whole of mankind once upon a time."

"When was that?"

"Exactly eighteen thousand and twenty years ago."

"How come we know about it today?"

The astrologer smiled indulgently. "My dear fellow, I did my dissertation on it."

The astrologer lit a cigarette. The hissing nucleus of the comet landed on his table. It had the shape of a star cut out of gold paper.

"You see, it is fond of me," said the astrologer with parental pride. "But now we ought to begin," he went on matter-of-factly. "First, I must know when you were born."

Martin told him the date and the astrologer pressed some buttons on his table. "In a moment we shall get the appropriate constellation. Meanwhile, let us move over to Libra. That is your sign. Did you know?"

"Yes."

"Libra will be approximately there," the astrologer pointed to the opposite side and released one of the levers by his table which set it in motion.

"Why does my fate have to be studied before Her Grace receives me?" asked Martin as they inched their way over the floor.

"Her Grace must know the man she meets in all his aspects. And if she knows his destiny, she can make what arrangements she pleases in the light of it."

"Have you ever seen Her Grace?" Martin inquired.

"I have never had the honor. Only a few people have ever come near her. So few, that personally I do not know anybody who has been in her presence."

"What sort of reputation has she got?"

The astrologer half rose to his feet in embarassment. He sat down. And stood up again. Then, with a solemn gesture, he raised his finger into the air.

"My friend, it is not right to touch upon sacred matters in everyday words, with an everyday mind. Her Grace . . . " he labored to find some words or some way of expressing himself. ". . . What more is there to say?" he ended, as if he had solved a difficult problem.

"Forgive me. — But isn't it strange that she wants to see me?"

"My dear fellow, neither you nor I should ask unnecessary questions. Besides, the fact that Her Grace wishes to see you does not necessarily mean that you will see Her."

Martin gaped with surprise.

"That did not occur to you, did it?" continued the astrologer with a smile. "Although that is what is most likely to happen."

"You think so?"

"I don't know. You must wait and see. But in any case you will have been honored for life."

Martin was about to ask another question, but the astrologer stopped him.

"Here we are," he announced. He looked up. The position of the stars had changed. "And this is your constellation."

A girl carrying refreshments came by. Martin helped himself to an open sandwich and a glass of some fizzy drink. The girl was handing him a paper napkin when it slipped out of her hand. Martin bent down to pick it up at the same time as she did.

"Don't touch anything — it is poisoned," the girl whispered. She walked away rapidly.

The astrologer was setting up various measuring instruments.

"Why don't you eat?" he asked.

Martin picked up the open sandwich. He hesitated.

"Aren't you hungry?" insisted the astrologer.

"I am hungry, but I don't eat poisoned food," Martin said curtly.

The astrologer put down his instruments and turned to Martin. "Poisoned . . . ? Who . . . ? It was she!" Suddenly he roared with laughter.

"What is so funny?" Martin was growing angry.

"The ideas she gets! My goodness!" The astrologer laughed so wildly that he nearly fell off his chair. Then he picked up a receiver and just managed to say "Service" before he was overcome by another fit of laughter.

The girl appeared right away.

"This is poisoned?" The astrologer pointed to Martin's snack, wiping the tears of laughter from his cheeks.

The girl stared ahead sullenly.

"Answer!"

"It was my idea," put in Martin.

"Really?" The astrologer turned to the girl: "Eat it."

She took the sandwich and swallowed it in one gulp. The astrologer handed her the glass, which she emptied with equal speed.

"You can go. — Do you know why they do it?" he addressed Martin again.

"No."

"Whatever is not eaten goes to the staff."

"I don't believe it."

"Of course it is so. I must admit that a morsel here and there really is poisoned, but such cases are kept to the bare minimum. And they occur only on certain days. It is all part of some experiments we are doing on the laws of probability."

"Then why did you force her to eat the sandwich?"

"Because to begin with today is not an experimental day, and then even if it were, I should not spoil a scientific test."

"So she is not going to die?"

"I must insist that from now on you stop interrupting me. Her Grace is waiting."

10

First they bathed Martin in a sumptuous pool full of floating balls. He played with them till the water splashed about. Then he tired of the game.

"There is no green ball here. I shall complain," he tried to bluster, but nobody took any notice of him.

A ceremonial robe was brought and the servants dressed Martin so quickly that he had no time to protest. A tall man in a white wig inspected Martin from all sides and then led him away.

They came to a hall of mirrors.

"I am Her Grace's second master of ceremonies," solemnly announced the man in the wig. "I shall now give you the necessary instructions."

"I do not need any," snapped Martin.

The master of ceremonies ignored his objection. "When you are led to the door of the crown chamber, you will bow to the waist and, remaining bowed, you will take fifty paces forward. If you hear a silver bell, you may straighten up, but then you will stand quite still. Is this part of the reception clear to you?"

"I thought we were in a hall of mirrors," said Martin, looking around him.

"You are not mistaken," answered the master of ceremonies.

"I am not mistaken? But I do not see myself in any of these mirrors."

"They are selective mirrors," the man in the wig informed him indulgently. "But now for the next part of the reception."

"I say," interrupted Martin, "I have been in the halls of the Third and the Second Law. I thought there would be a First Law as well."

"The First Law is Her Grace. But that is a mystery beyond the grasp of a mere human. This mystery is expounded by the secret officials of the First Law, though of course it can never be explained completely," he added with the smile of an initiate. "But that is something we ordinary mortals need not worry about. As far as we are concerned, there are two Laws and one Mystery — Her Grace," the master of ceremonies said, making a deep bow. As he did so, his wig fell off. He pushed it to the wall with his foot. At that moment another courtier rushed into the hall.

"This fellow," he said, pointing to Martin, "has been chosen as Her Grace's lover," he announced breathlessly. "It will be here in writing any minute. I have just seen the original order at the calligraphers. They are working on it as fast as they can."

The master of ceremonies clutched his head in affected horror. "Lover! Him? For heaven's sake, what are you waiting for? Sound the alarm!"

The courtier rushed to a handle on the wall and whirled it frantically. The screaming of a siren immediately filled the hall of mirrors with servants.

"Bathe him! Change his clothes! Lace linen! Oriental perfumes!" the master of ceremonies shouted in frenzy.

"They have bathed me already," Martin raged.

"Again! Something might have been overlooked!"

"Out of the question," cried Martin, but he was instantly submerged beneath the servants' bodies.

Martin was thrown into the water once more, but this time it had flowers and goldfish floating in it. A whole army of servants soaped and rinsed him under the supervision of several courtiers.

"Now rub him with precious ointments," ordered the master of ceremonies some time later.

The barbers and the masseurs set to work.

"They did not wipe me dry," grumbled Martin. "I'll get a rash."

"Linen! Suit!" The master of ceremonies directed the next stage of Martin's preparations. "Perfumes."

"I haven't got any shoes on yet," Martin pointed out.

"Shoes!" cried the master of ceremonies.

"Now I'm sweating all over," remarked Martin.

The master of ceremonies stopped as if he had been struck by lightning. "You are sweating?"

Then all at once he plunged into a wild burst of activity. "Another bath! Quickly! Change his clothes! New linen and suit!" Nobody even heard Martin's protests.

At last Martin was ready. The courtiers checked every detail once more.

"Let us go," said the master of ceremonies finally. They came out into a long corridor lit by a few candles. On the walls hung precious tapestries representing pastoral games.

"I have not had time to give you all the instructions. Anyway, the whole style of the reception will be quite different now. At least you will not get it mixed up. But the first stage will remain the same. Only instead of the silver bell, a golden one will ring. You will straighten up with your eyes fixed on the throne. Then Her Grace will make a sign with her hand and you will kneel. Next, Her Grace will probably speak. You will approach on tiptoe in a curve leading to the left side of the throne steps. Then . . . ''

"I say," interrupted Martin, "what does Her Grace look like?"

"What has that got to do with you?" the master of ceremonies flared up. "Here we are," he whispered. "The waiting room." Martin only shrugged.

An enormously tall door opened wide. "You will wait here until the first master of ceremonies comes to fetch you. And then . . . follow the instructions to the letter, please." He bowed and left.

Martin found that the waiting room was the large hall of a railroad station, full of hurrying people and the sounds of trains arriving and leaving. The smell of smoke and the dirty tiles in the corridors gave the finishing touch to the atmosphere. An anonymous voice kept calling out train numbers and the names of stations Martin did not know. He set out down the main corridor, which was lined with benches, most of them occupied by passengers and their luggage. At last he found a free place next to a man in ragged clothes who had fallen asleep there. He was half laying along the seat and making hoarse sounds. When Martin sat down, the man partly opened one eye.

"Where to?"

"To Her Grace," replied Martin gloomily.

"Lover?" asked the tramp.

"How did you know?"

"It's in all the papers."

"Is that so?"

"Yes. Have you ever been there before?"

"No."

The tramp was about to say something, but he stopped. He tugged at Martin's sleeve. "There he is now, coming to fetch you."

The first master of ceremonies, dressed all in gold, was standing by the main entrance to the hall. He was a man who radiated perfect self-confidence, combined with some higher awareness. For an instant Martin felt he had seen him before somewhere, but he dismissed the idea straight away as obviously absurd. The master of ceremonies struck the ground three times with his staff and in a ringing voice announced through all the loudspeakers in the halls: "Martin is to present himself immediately to Her Grace. I repeat — Martin . . . "

People came running from all sides and formed a dense crowd, leaving only a narrow lane in the middle.

"Wouldn't you like to take my place?" whispered Martin.

The tramp sleepily shook his head in commiseration. Martin rose and walked slowly down the lane between the people. They inspected him curiously, smiled at him, several brought out notebooks with requests for an autograph. Here and there some applause broke out and gradually swelled in volume. Martin walked on, uncertainly bowing left and right. At last he reached the master of ceremonies and disappeared through a door that immediately closed behind him.

In the corridor the master of ceremonies looked Martin up and down, coughed, glanced at his watch, and said in an unofficial voice, "In forty-five seconds I shall announce you. Are you ready?"

"Yes," growled Martin.

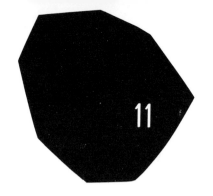

11

Martin bowed, but not as deeply as the instructions prescribed. Then he walked approximately fifty paces with his head only slightly bent and, without waiting for the golden bell to ring, looked up.

It was an immensely long hall, shining with light, filled with rare pieces of furniture, carpets, chandeliers, and mural paintings. Somewhere far ahead, under a broad canopy on a raised dais, stood the throne. The person sitting on it was difficult to make out.

Martin advanced a few more paces. Then again. And once more. His eyes bulging, he came right up to the throne steps and stopped there.

"Where is Her Grace?" he forced out in a strangled voice.

"I am Her Grace," answered the little girl of about eight who was sitting on the throne. She wore a regal robe and had a crown glittering with jewels on her head, a scepter in her right hand and in her left an imperial orb.

"That is not possible," whispered Martin.

The little girl gave a constrained smile. "Why not?"

"They told me . . . your courtiers . . . they said . . . that you are . . ."

"Etiquette requires you to call me Your Grace," the child admonished him with a smile.

"They said that I . . ."

"Would you help me lay down my orb and scepter?" asked the girl. "They are rather heavy."

Martin was about to mount the steps to the throne, when the little girl rose abruptly to her feet.

"It seems that you were not given adequate instructions," she said crossly.

"Am I doing something wrong?" Martin was taken aback.

"Everything," she replied. "Now, for instance, you should be kneeling."

Martin knelt down.

"Your instructor will be severely punished," declared the girl.

"It is not his fault. I am a very bad pupil," Martin tried to save the situation. "Your Grace," he added quickly. He took the scepter and the orb out of her hands and looked around where to put them down.

"I'll put them on the ground for the time being. Let us hope they do not roll away," Martin decided. The little girl sat down with dignity and Martin followed suit.

The child looked at him critically for a while. "Do you know who is the only person allowed to sit on these steps?" she asked after a pause.

"No, I don't"

"The jester," she said with a touch of contempt.

"Really? How interesting. But I don't mind."

"So it seems. — A moment ago you were about to say something," she reminded him.

"Oh, yes. They told me that Her Grace had chosen me for her . . . friend. Well, if we are to be friends, we must behave in a friendly manner," said Martin.

"What you have just said sounds like very bad information. But I think you have somewhat modified the original, correct instructions."

"What did you say?" Martin rose to his feet.

"Sit down," said the girl, pale with anger. "You were chosen to be my lover. Isn't that right?"

"This is going too far," exclaimed Martin.

The little girl suddenly broke into merry, childish laughter. "Take off my crown."

Martin went on glaring sullenly at the ceiling.

"Please," she begged in a wheedling little voice.

Her laughter finally conquered Martin. He took off her crown and laid it beside the other things on the carpet.

And now tell me a story," she curled up on the throne and gazed at Martin expectantly.

"What about?"

"About the sun. What does it look like?"

"A big yellow eye in the sky. It gives heat and light," said Martin.

"You have not told me much," she said after a while. "And what about the world?"

"You want me to tell you about the world?"

"Yes."

"I say, I know a lovely fairy tale about the sun," Martin suddenly had an idea.

"That is rather disturbing at your age. You should have more mature thoughts," she replied dryly.

Now it was Martin's turn to laugh. "Tell me, why did they send me to you?" he asked at last, full of good humor.

The little girl got up and held out her left hand. Martin offered her his right arm and they descended the steps. "We are going to make love. You are no fun to be with," the girl said severely.

When they reached the floor, the little girl stretched back

her arms: "One, two, three!" And then, jumping rhythmi-
cally up and down she sang a nursery rhyme:

> A handsome prince came riding
> To woo a young princess
> As soon as he had wed her
> He carried her away.

Martin picked up the rhythm of her movements and by the
time she got to the second stanza, he was singing with her.

> As soon as he had wed her
> He carried her away
> Far across the ocean
> To his father's great castle.

So they skipped and shrilled all the way to the door of the
chamber and then back again to the throne.

"Faster. And louder," cried the girl.

> Far across the ocean
> To his father's great castle
> There he swore to love her
> Until the darkest grave.

They behaved more and more wildly until the floor and the
things around them shook.

"Are you enjoying this?" cried the little girl.

"Tremendously! But won't someone come and tell us off
for making all this noise?"

"No one is allowed to. This is a matter of state."

> There he swore to love her
> Until the darkest grave . . .

"Do you know how it goes on?" shouted the girl.

"No, I don't."

"Then we'll just sing la-la-la, shall we?"

> There he swore to love her
> Until the darkest grave
> La-la, la-la, la-la
> La-la, la-la, la-la.

"I can't go on," said the girl and sat down on the steps of the throne. "I am quite out of breath."

"Take a rest." Martin was panting heavily.

"Thank you. You made a great lover."

"What did you say?"

"I said you made a great lover. As a companion you are not much good, but you do know how to make love."

Martin could not suppress a smile. "Thank you for the compliment. Now at last I see . . . Believe me, I didn't know what to think."

"Don't talk about it. It is improper."

"Shall we . . . ?"

"I can't just now. My financial council will be here any moment."

"So I have the honor to take my leave, Your Grace," Martin said with a smile.

At last the little girl recovered her breath. "No, wait a moment. Don't you want to see the fruit of our love?"

Martin gulped.

The girl led him to a kind of slot machine standing by the wall. She pressed a button and the next instant a screaming infant, carefully wrapped in cellophane, fell out. The girl tore off the wrapping and inspected the baby.

"How do you like it?" she asked Martin.

"A very pretty child."

"It is a little boy — your son. I have a lot of children by now, but I think I shall be very fond of this one. What would you like to call him?"

"I don't know. I'll leave it up to you."

"That's right. But now I must give you permission to withdraw."

She held out her hand and Martin found a child's ring with a little yellow stone lying in his palm.

"A souvenir," said the little girl and, before Martin could protest, she disappeared through a door hidden in the wall.

Martin slipped the ring circumspectly under the heavy carpet and slowly left the throne room.

12

The master of ceremonies took Martin by the shoulder and whispered confidentially: "Run for it! You are to be arrested any moment."

"Why?"

"You know that all Her Grace's lovers have to be silenced, don't you?"

Martin burst through the tall door and found himself back in the waiting room. He sped through it and rushed out into the street. Somewhere behind him the siren of a police car started to wail.

Martin quickened his pace. The people in the streets were stopping; some were waving to encourage him. But still the siren came closer and closer. Martin felt his heart thumping. At last the car caught up with him and drove alongside. In the midst of the policemen sat the master of ceremonies, smiling.

"You will have to go faster than that. You don't want to disgrace yourself, do you?" he said affably.

Martin tried to put on another spurt, but the car kept level with him.

"Aren't you thirsty?" asked the master of ceremonies. "There is a café over there. Go and have a drink, and we'll wait for you here."

Martin suddenly sprinted across the sidewalk, jumped

over a low fence, and ran into a park. He looked back. The car was at his heels. People came running from all sides. Martin raced up to a broad tree in the middle of the lawn and leaned against its trunk. The car stopped a few paces in front of him.

"Is that all?" inquired the master of ceremonies.

"Go to blazes," snapped Martin.

People had gathered in a wide semicircle around them. Some were sitting down and getting ready to picnic in the grass.

"That is the end. He has given up!" cried the master of ceremonies to the groups of onlookers.

The people began to whistle, boo, and throw paper pellets at Martin.

"I will not run! I will defend myself!" bellowed Martin.

This was greeted with spontaneous applause. The master of ceremonies, too, was obviously pleased; he made a sign to the policemen and they got out of the car. He gave a signal and pistols appeared in their hands. At the next signal, they took aim.

"Well, do something," the master of ceremonies challenged him.

Martin took off a shoe and hurled it with all his might at one of the policemen; then he did the same with the other one. He looked about; a big, dead branch was lying nearby. Martin gripped it with both hands and set upon the policemen with it; he struck out blindly, hitting all of them practically at the same time. They stood motionless.

The master of ceremonies, who had been looking on pensively, said to Martin, "I say, it is about time you let them be. They can't do anything to you without an order and I am afraid I have forgotten how the order to fire goes.''

Martin threw the branch away. ''Anyway, I'm tired.'' He sat down on the ground.

''Arrest him!'' suddenly cried the master of ceremonies and the policemen rushed at Martin. This move pleased the spectators, who welcomed it with cheers. The master of ceremonies bowed modestly to all sides. Martin jumped to his feet and, crouching down, fled into the nearest street. Before his pursuers came to their senses, he was thrusting his way between the passersby. Then he noticed an open sewer and without a moment's hesitation he lowered himself below ground.

He found he was in a high, vaulted passage, which smelled intolerably of mothballs. Martin ran up to an underground intersection, where he was stopped by a policeman directing the traffic. Martin shifted impatiently from one foot to the other.

''You just wait there nicely,'' the policeman cautioned him, ''or you will have to pay a fine.''

Martin nodded and glanced back. None of his pursuers were in sight.

''Are you on the run?'' asked the policeman sympathtically.

''Yes.''

''In that case, you will have to register. Take the third passage to the right and then the first to the left.''

''Will they help me there!''

''Of course. You will fill out a questionnaire, attach a photograph and a stamp, and you're free.''

The policeman signaled with his arms and Martin broke into a run. The pungent smell of mothballs began to grow fainter.

At the place indicated, Martin found a board door blocked by a group of men engaged in lively conversation.

"You have to get in line," one of them said to Martin, who was trying to force his way to the door.

"But they are after me," Martin protested impatiently. "Can't you see? They're at my heels."

"You have to get in line," repeated the man with unshakable certitude.

Martin extricated himself from the bunch of people and set out at a sharp pace along an empty passage. They stared after him in confused indignation.

This passage was somewhat narrower, the raised sidewalk hardly a step wide. In the middle ran a dark stream with all kinds of refuse floating in it — animal carcasses, sewage, chunks of sodden books, and from time to time even pieces of human limbs appeared. Martin quickened his pace. The sound of his steps reverberated along the walls of the passage. It grew darker and darker. When he had walked for many hours, Martin saw in the distance a large cave with a crowd of human figures in it. By the time he reached them he was exhausted from his march, the darkness, and the damp chill of the passage. The cave turned out to be an immense artificial grotto, with a thick, foul-smelling lake at the bottom. Its shores stretched away out of sight into the dark distance. Throngs of people were strolling along the edge of the stagnant water. There was also a ferryboat anchored there, and a man with a dark blue, peaked army cap was standing by it. He was holding the boat on a rope wound around his wrist.

"Can you take me away from here?" Martin accosted him.

The man glanced at him impassively. "Do you have money?"

Martin showed him what cash he had.

"That is not legal tender here," the man remarked softly.

"Well, what am I to do then?" blurted out Martin.

The man shrugged. "Go and earn some."

"But they are after me, don't you see? I have to get to the other side."

"And what do you think all these people here are doing?" the man nodded towards the strolling crowds.

"Are they all waiting for the ferry?" gasped Martin.

"Naturally. They make money, save, and come here to keep their goal in sight."

"How often do you go across?"

The man stopped to think. "In the last four years I have taken the boat out at least three times."

"Three times? How much does the trip cost?"

"Ten thousand."

"Ten thousand!" exclaimed Martin. "But surely, that is impossible."

"It can just as well be five or twenty thousand. That depends on how you behave. If you shout, or make a scene, you will pay fifty thousand," the man said apathetically.

"Are you the manager here?" Martin tried a different approach.

"I am the ferryman," replied the man and turned away.

The sharp trill of a whistle pierced the air.

Martin quickly pushed his way to where the crowd was densest. Everyone was now making for one of the broad passages that opened into the cave.

"What is going on?" whispered Martin to a man he found by his side.

"The start of the shift," answered the man, vigorously elbowing his way forward.

Martin kept behind his back until they came to a space beneath a vaulted ceiling, which was slowly dripping water. Some of the walls were rather damaged, the masonry battered or falling, the plaster crumbling away. Some lichen, which had settled in the cracks, gave off a dull green phosphorescent glow.

Somewhere in the front an order was given and the people took up certain positions. At the next command, they began to move. Their movements were of various kinds, but each was constantly repeated. Martin's neighbor always did three knee bends, stretched his arms back twice, and finished with a forward bend. He went on doing this over and over again. When he noticed Martin looking at him, he started chatting.

"I am not as good at this work as I used to be," he grumbled. "They'll have to give me something easier to do. Once upon a time I used to fulfill the highest norms and still managed to spend the night out on the tiles with the boys. But now I'm beginning to feel it in my bones."

A man came up to Martin. "Are you new here?" he asked. "Yes."

"Are you skilled? Do you have any experience?" "No."

The man nodded. "Never mind. We'll find you something. Of course you won't be making much to start with, you know. But in time I'll get you trained."

The man pondered a while. "I've got it! What do you think of this: Arms forward, sideways, up — jump? Good, isn't it? But you will have to go and do the jump over there. Here the ground is giving way a bit. Well, try it!"

Martin stretched his arms forward, sideways and up, moved a few steps away, and jumped.

"Good," said the man, pleased. "I told you we should

find something. You are under my personal supervision. Right, now go ahead!''

Martin started drilling, and the supervisor moved away.

''I say,'' Martin turned to his neighbor. ''I've got to get ten thousand. Do you happen to know of anybody who would lend it to me?''

''I need three,'' replied the man. ''But I think I shall retire before I get them together. So I always have two possibilities open to me, you see. I just happen to be lucky, that's all. But ten thousand is too much.''

''Do those above ever come down here?'' another thought occurred to Martin.

''Naturally.''

''I was wondering about inspections.''

''Naturally. You have to be registered, otherwise you won't stay here long.''

In the evening, a good many of the inhabitants gathered in an underground theater. There were no seats there, only a single chair set out in front. It had a tattered screen hanging on the wall above it and a battered loud speaker standing by its side. After a brief pause, one of the supervisors climbed on to the chair and announced the program: ''Can number sixty-four.''

The public clapped enthusiastically.

''What does that mean?'' Martin asked a young woman who was leaning against the wall.

''It is canned laughter. It seems that at one time they had comedy shows here, and they used to play tapes of laughter with them, so that people would have more fun. But then it turned out that the shows did not have to be put on at all.

People have only to hear laughter and they laugh too.''

"Nonsense," said Martin.

"You'll see."

The tremor of a light laugh came through the air. The audience became attentive.

"Sixty-four has a rather slow beginning, but then it is excellent,'' whispered the young woman. "Have you got a cigarette?''

Martin offered her one and lit it. Again there came a rustle of gentle laughter.

"What are you doing after the show?'' the woman asked softly.

"I haven't made up my mind."

"Maybe we should sleep together. But the way I like it is when there is no hurry about it. I just love to press on, but then most men are through right away and a lot of them even stay inside.''

The first gust of laughter flew through the hall and very slowly died away. The public was beginning to enjoy itself.

"Do you like to go from behind? You can get at the breasts better that way, can't you?''

Martin nodded in agreement. Another wave of laughter was taken up by the audience and swept through the vault. The young woman laughed.

"I have to feel a man as deep as possible, otherwise it's no good. The deeper the better,'' she added matter-of-factly.

Martin was beginning to smile too by now. Rather woodenly, but still with enormous relief.

At the next outburst of canned sound, the whole hall rang with unbridled mirth.

When Martin calmed down a little, he turned to the young woman. "Have you said everything you had to say, or do you still have more bombshells in reserve?"

"You misunderstood me," protested the young woman. "I am a virgin."

The vault re-echoed with another shriek of laughter.

"Of course," agreed Martin. "A moral virgin."

The people around them were rolling about, helpless with laughter.

Martin moved a step away from the girl.

"Well, this will not do," a familiar voice said near him.

Martin turned and saw the master of ceremonies with a group of policemen.

"You are supposed to be fleeing through thick and thin, and instead of that you go to the movies. And what is more, you molest young women," continued the master of ceremonies angrily.

Martin fought his way through the crowd of spectators toward the exit.

"I have not been molesting anybody," he growled back.

"Is that so? Bring the woman," ordered the master of ceremonies, following Martin.

By the exit the crowd was less dense and Martin broke into a run. The regular thudding of boots followed him.

"I hereby open the trial," puffed the master of ceremonies, out of breath with running. "What is your name, witness?"

"Juliet," declared the young woman, who was being dragged along by several policemen.

"Did the accused molest you?" the master of ceremonies continued without slackening his pace.

"What do you mean?" asked the witness.

"Did he insult you?"

"Yes. He said I was a moral virgin."

"The jury will retire for deliberation," decided the master of ceremonies. Still running, the policemen came together in a huddle. One of them stumbled over a dead rat.

"Please keep in step," the master of ceremonies admonished them. "Every slip may vitiate your verdict."

Martin saw the underground lake before him. The ferryman was still standing by his boat.

"Have you come to a decision?" cried the master of ceremonies at his back.

"Just a minute," came from the group.

"Be quick about it!" bellowed the master of ceremonies.

"Guilty," cried the group with one voice.

"You will be deported . . ." began the master of ceremonies, but he did not finish.

Martin gathered all his strength, sprang, and dived into the fetid lake.

"To the boat!" ordered the master of ceremonies. The group ran alongside the lake towards the ferryman. With powerful strokes, Martin moved away from the shore. The liquid in which he was swimming was slimily tepid.

"I ought to swim below the surface," Martin realized. He gave a quick glance back. His pursuers had just reached the boat. The ferryman made some objection, but he was pushed aside so roughly that he fell to the ground. The men jumped into the boat and seized the oars. The master of ceremonies took his stand in the middle of the ferry, holding a revolver in his outstretched hand.

"Ready — Steady —." A shot rang out, and the crew

pulled at the oars. Two more shots followed in quick succession. Fragments of brick from the vaulted ceiling fell into the water near Martin.

"Bad start!" snarled the master of ceremonies in the boat. "Can't you pull together? Don't oblige me to take strong measures. Again! Ready — Steady —." Another shot roared out somewhere near the ceiling.

Martin noticed an inlet where the lake flowed out into one of the passages. He rapidly changed course and swam with powerful strokes into the passage. A few more strokes, and he felt the ground under his feet. He scrambled up on shore and broke into a run. But he felt that his strength was failing. He could hear the peculiarly distorted echo of the master of ceremonies' voice: "One — two — three, one — two — three . . . "

Martin's run turned into a walk and grew slower and slower. He began to trip over his feet.

"One — two — three . . ."

"I have a lead," Martin calculated, "so I can take a little nap. Anyway, everything around here stinks . . . "

Martin did not come to until much later. He was in jail, his legs fettered to the wall by two strong chains. Nearby, some silver-grey mice were scurrying about, but they were only clockwork toys. When they stopped, a jailer came in with a key and began to wind them up one by one.

"How did I get here?" Martin asked him.

"They brought you in during the night," answered the jailer, without pausing in his work; he barely glanced at Martin.

"Why are you doing that? I am not afraid of mice. Not even live ones," said Martin.

"That makes no difference. Everything has to be run properly. A prison without mice would have no atmosphere."

"What is going to happen to me?"

"Your execution will take place in an hour."

"Execution?"

"I hope you will cooperate. People must cooperate," muttered the jailer.

"I shall do nothing of the sort."

"You will," the jailer assured him. "The doctor will be here in a moment and he'll give you an injection to make you cooperate."

"I want rum," cried Martin. "And a girl!"

"You have only one last wish. Well, what will it be?"

"Dynamite."

The jailer sighed. "If you don't cooperate, your pension will go to the state and they won't put up a statue to you."

"What statue?"

"A bronze one. You will stand in the castle avenue among Her Grace's other favorites."

A doctor came in and with the jailer's help gave the prisoner the injection. Martin put up only a feeble struggle, merely as a matter of principle rather than with much determination, so he did not manage to prevent the doctor from performing his task.

"That will be ten pieces of gold," said the doctor. Martin paid and the doctor left.

"Please tell me how I am to die," Martin begged the jailer.

"There is a rock near here from which you will be hurled off the face of the earth."

"Where to?"

"Into eternal chaos. In the old days it used to be called hell."

"Thank you."

"Don't mention it. And now I'll leave you alone." The jailer gave Martin a facetious wink. "Have a good time."

A girl dressed up as a ballet dancer came in; her whole attire consisted of three roses and long light brown hair.

"I love you," Martin addressed her in a surly voice. He had been expecting a brunette.

"Although we have known each other a comparatively short time, I must confess that I, too, feel affection for you. Considerable affection," said the girl.

"I cannot believe that such great good fortune could be mine," said Martin. "Please take off your things and make yourself at home," he continued affectedly.

"Darling . . ." the girl threw herself into Martin's arms. "I feel as if all this were only a dream."

Martin took her in his arms.

"You have taken the first of my roses," whispered the girl a moment later.

Martin again encircled her with his strong arms.

"You have taken the second of my roses," she gasped with sultry breath.

Now Martin caught her up in a crushing embrace.

"You have taken the third of my roses," she said at last, swooning with pleasure. "What is to become of me now, my love?"

Martin shrugged.

"What will happen to your pension, darling?"

"It's yours," said Martin.

She kissed him on his bare chest. "Thanks."

The jailer appeared in the doorway, smiling uneasily.

"Amnesty?" asked Martin.

"Forgive me for disturbing you, but the executioner is waiting," the jailer reported apologetically. "He has a game of chess arranged for the afternoon, and he would like to get this over and done with."

"I was just leaving, anyway," said the girl. She got up and dressed.

Martin was led out on to a high mountain topped with a small plateau that stretched out over a deep precipice, jutting into the air like a broken bridge.

The executioner was an affable old fellow with a perpetually smoking pipe in his mouth. On the way he chattered to Martin, explaining that he intended to change his name when he retired. When they got to the top of the mountain, he had to fight with his whole body against the strong wind that was continually pushing him to the edge of the plateau.

"Please catch me!" he cried when another gust of wind flung him to the very edge. Martin caught him by a coattail and drew him back to safety.

"Thank you. Think what a tragedy it would be for you if I fell off there instead of you." The little old man got up and again the wind started to push him to the edge. He struggled valiantly to regain lost ground.

"I don't see that it would be a tragedy for me," said Martin.

"Oh, you don't?" the old man wheezed with exertion. "Help!"

Martin caught him once more and got him to safety.

"I am a grandmaster in chess, you know, but I have to let

other people win to get anyone at all to play with me. Catch me!''

''And that is the last time,'' said Martin, dragging the little old man back to the center of the plateau. ''I am not going to go on hauling you about.''

The old man now lay flat on the ground to escape the force of the wind. ''All right, if you are not going to take care of me, I shall execute you and that will be that. We could have had a nice little chat, we could have prolonged your life a bit, but you are a rough, unsociable fellow. Hand me the pole lying over there and go and stand on the edge.''

''What are you going to do?'' asked Martin, handing the old man a long, thin pole of fir wood.

''I shall give you a push and you will fall down,'' said the little old man menacingly.

Martin went and stood directly above the precipice.

''Do you play chess?'' piped the little old man, avoiding Martin's eye.

Martin roared with laughter. ''It would be nice to play with me, wouldn't it? You wouldn't have to lose to me.''

''You are an impertinent, rude little boy,'' the old man was fuming with rage.

Martin laughed more and more wildly; as if the wind were part of his laughter, as if he were part of the wind.

''Go on, push,'' cried Martin. ''I feel exceedingly light.''

''I shall do nothing of the sort,'' scolded the old man. ''I am to do everything for you, while you do nothing for me? I shall do nothing of the sort.''

''Push me,'' laughed Martin, ''or I shall write a personal letter of complaint to Her Grace.''

"No. You will live a bit longer. In fact, I'll let you go on living for good," threatened the executioner.

"Push me, or I'll fly away," said Martin exultantly.

The wind grew stronger and stronger.

"I'm warning you for the last time," shouted Martin. Then he felt the tip of the pole touching his chest and feebly pushing him off the plateau.

"Push a bit harder, executioner," Martin spurred him on.

The pressure slightly increased and Martin felt that he was slowly losing his balance.

PART THREE

13

Martin hurdled past the rock, which soon disappeared from his sight. Shortly afterwards, the wind that was lashing round him died down. Then the pressure in his body, which was making him perform various involuntary movements and causing his ears to hum, vanished too. And quite suddenly there was absolute silence. Martin found himself floating in a kind of serene light. He felt immensely exalted.

His first idea was to stand on his feet again, but to his surprise he saw that he was already upright. He did not feel quite sure, however, so he decided to try to lie down; but immediately he found that again without making any movement he was lying flat.

"That is funny," said Martin. But strangely enough he did not hear his own words. He clapped, to verify this state of affairs. This time he not only did not hear any sound, he did not even feel his palms touching. Yet he saw positively that they struck together.

He looked around, glanced up above, peered down at his feet, but everywhere there was only that pale, grayish brightness.

"I must be standing on something," thought Martin. He stamped and felt that he moved, and also that he remained in the same place.

His gay mood left him. He was afraid that he would be frightened. He waited for a while, but the fear did not come.

"I'll die of hunger," it suddenly occurred to him. "And of thirst." But this thought did not, on the whole, upset him. Indeed, his feeling was actually one of indifference. It was not a passive recklessness, however, but rather a kind of magnanimous void.

"All right," he said soundlessly after a while. "But what shall I do?" He thought hard but could find no answer except to go somewhere and find somebody or at least something. Unfortunately, walking did not bring any change at all and, besides, he suspected that there was no creature or object anywhere about. He did a few knee bends, to see what would happen, but he could not tell if he brought his trunk down to his legs or his legs up to his trunk. He gave up.

"I must not panic." He went on moving his lips, but there was nothing left to say. The profound void inside him began to fill up with something. As if he were breathing in the grayish brightness around him.

His painful sensation was infused with a beneficent assent. For a moment they were one, and then everything vanished. He felt he was beginning to move with an infinitely gentle motion — as if he were floating, without speed and without direction. Gradually he was becoming someone or some-thing entirely different, as if he existed outside himself. At the same time he started to grow outwards; he became the earth, the planets, the sun, the universe. His limits were expanding, he was becoming more and more complete, ap-proaching the outermost bounds. He had the impression that he was taking on the shape of an idea, or maybe an explosion of light.

"Dear friend!" Martin sensed the familiar voice some-where nearby.

"Dear friend, wait just a tiny second! I'll be right with you," entreated the voice.

Martin opened his eyes. The master of ceremonies was standing by his side. This time he was alone and smiling uncertainly.

"You must come back immediately. There has been a terrible mistake. Your execution is invalid. The executioner got the cell numbers mixed up. Please try to understand, he is an old man and he does get us into this kind of a mess occasionally. We shall put everything right. If you like, the old fellow will offer you his apologies."

Martin gave a chuckle. "I say, what is the matter with me? Am I not dead yet?"

"No. But you are extremely near it."

"Where am I, anyway?"

"Don't you remember? You are falling, of course. And by this time, my friend, you are going at a dizzying speed. You know the law of free fall, don't you?

"Am I in a void?"

"Yes."

"I should not have said so. But if it is true, what can you do for me? Will you give me a parachute?"

"Please don't joke about it. Your situation is critical."

"Now I look at you closely," Martin began from another angle, "I notice that from time to time you look rather like a man I met recently. His name was Abel."

"Really?" stuttered the master of ceremonies. "What a curious coincidence, isn't it? But I am not Abel."

"I don't know. Besides, I am quite happy here," concluded Martin.

"But for heaven's sake, think of the end that is awaiting

you. And that end is approaching at a fearful speed. My friend I implore you, come back with me at once!''

''I am not thinking about the end. I do not have to think about anything any more, because everything is inside me. Even that end of mine. Especially that.''

''What a preposterous error! Don't you realize that you are deluding yourself?''

''How strange,'' mused Martin. ''Even you . . . are . . . part . . . ''

''Be quiet! You are sick. Look, I've got a pill here. It is a lead compound of some kind. You must swallow it.''

Martin smiled. ''I always know beforehand what you are going to say. And what I shall answer. I know the whole of this meeting between us. It is rather a bore for me to have to go through it step by step, when in a way the whole thing is over and done with.''

''You are in delirium!''

''No. I am in a void, as you called it.''

''My friend, do try to understand — I have to bring you back, or . . . ''

''Or?''

The master of ceremonies waved it aside. ''I had rather not talk about it. Besides, it is you we are concerned about.''

Close by them, a plaster bust of the sort found in schools and museums suddenly came into view.

''What is that?'' Martin turned to the master of ceremonies.

''It is starting to rain. Pay no attention.''

The bust slowly floated downwards. Other objects emerged above it. From the distance they looked like parts of a rococo costume.

''It looks a bit like you,'' said Martin, pointing to the bust.

"May I call you Martin?" began the master of ceremonies.

"No. That name is no longer enough."

"Come back with me! You will get a fabulous salary, we shall give you a villa and a chauffeur-driven car. What do you say?"

"I don't want it."

"You will get two or three high decorations. You will be able to go out among people with ribbons on your breast."

"You are talking nonsense."

"Very well. In that case I shall tell you something that will shatter you. I wanted to spare you, but it is not possible."

"Go on."

"You, my friend, are standing on your head! Everything in you is topsy turvy, your whole world is upside down. What you are seeing are the delusions of a man on the point of collapse. And your fall will be catastrophic. There, now you know."

"I shall burst like a puffed up frog," added Martin softly.

"I'll tell you something: we'll compromise. We shall go and have a quiet talk somewhere and you will not give me your decision till afterwards."

The master of ceremonies took Martin's arm, and the next moment they were standing outside the door of an office that bore the sign: "A.B.L. Central Management."

"One of my branches," explained the master of ceremonies as he opened the door.

Martin entered a large room filled with heavy mahagony furniture and a great number of pictures. Through a glass wall he could see a garden where a small child was playing with a butterfly.

"I didn't know . . . " Martin turned to his companion.

But the man who came into the room behind him was no longer the master of ceremonies but Abel.

"What didn't you know?" Abel asked.

"I didn't know you were married," said Martin mechanically.

He examined his host, who was once again wearing a perfectly tailored suit. The hole on the left side of the breast had evidently healed. He was holding a Turkish cigarette with a gold mouthpiece in his right hand; its smoke smelled of incense.

"I am not married. That child is me when I was young. It is a kind of sentimental memento. But it is very dear to me."

"Naturally," remarked Martin. "Permit me to ask. Am I still falling?"

The man stubbed out his cigarette. "Let us say that you have gained a little time. That is quite enough. And now to come to your business. We have received a bill for some masks. Was that necessary?"

"Absolutely. Otherwise I should have been recognized right away."

"Where are the masks now?"

"I lost them somewhere on the way."

"That was very careless of you. You do not seem to have much sense of financial responsibility. Also, I gave you a certain amount of money in ready cash."

Martin felt in his pocket. "This is what I have left."

The man took the money and carefully counted it, smoothing out each crumpled piece of paper. He mumbled some figures as he did so.

"I should say that you have changed quite a bit since my last visit," remarked Martin.

"You have changed, too," replied the man.

"I have been changed," snapped Martin.

They looked at each other. The man sighed.

"I am responsible to the board of directors," he said with a touch of apology. "By the way, how did your mission work out? Did you have any success?"

"I am ready to give you my report."

"Yes. You must type it out. You will use white, unlined paper, size eight by eleven, and make two copies. Try to get the best paper you can, preferably rag stock, but it must not be glossy. The dimensions are very important. Certain members of the board would simply refuse to read it otherwise. Is that clear? Eight by eleven."

The man finished counting the money and went up to one of the pictures on the wall. It was a still life with an onion and a pipe. Abel turned the picture back and behind it there appeared a safe, with a pale boy sitting inside it.

"That is me when I was eight years old," he remarked modestly. He laid the money beside the boy, who reached out and began to fold one of the pieces of paper into the shape of a dove. Abel shut the safe.

"How interesting," said Martin. "Does every picture have a safe containing your past behind it?"

Abel gave a gratified smile. "It's my hobby." He turned back another picture, revealing a young girl who was singing a wistful song in some strange language.

"My first love," said Abel and he shut the safe.

Behind the next picture there was a rocky landscape with a path winding away toward some distant mountains.

"This is where I spent my youth," sighed Abel. "Do you find this interesting?"

"Immensely."

Behind the following picture, there was a thunderbolt flashing in the darkness.

"This thunderbolt," said Abel, "changed the whole course of my life. But that is too private a story." He shut the safe. "We could go on like this," he waved towards the other pictures, "but for someone who is not in the know, it is merely a disparate collection." Clearly, the show was over. "But now for your case. How soon can you have the report ready?"

"You must be aware of the fact that I shall not write anything of the sort."

"You won't?" Abel drew himself up. "You refuse to submit a report about a journey on which you were officially sent?" His voice sounded more and more menacing. "You had better think it over carefully!"

"I should love to know," drawled Martin, "what you can do to me. Now that I am well on the way to smashing myself on the ground somewhere." Martin sat down on the sofa and gave Abel a mocking look. "The fact is, sir, that I am dying. So what are you going to do? Kill me? Oh no, you won't do that. It is the other one who does that, isn't it?" Martin continued with amusement.

"You are rather naive," growled Abel.

"Maybe. Sit down, I'd like to tell you something."

Abel complied.

"You know," began Martin. "I see your . . . let us say duality. — Let me finish. — I even see the necessity of everything that has happened to me. It could not have been any other way — that race alongside the fence. But now something has changed."

"It certainly has. In a moment you will hit the very bottom."

"Of course, there are moments the end of which not even you may live to see."

"I haven't got time to sit here philosophizing with you," objected Abel in an uncertain voice.

"If you had any faith in yourself at all, we should not be sitting here opposite one another like this."

Abel sprang to his feet. "Go back!" he said in a changed voice.

"There . . . into the light?"

"Yes, there. It will be best for you to go on floating in that . . . space. I shall give you a pair of little balloons to take with you, and they will keep you in a safe sphere."

"I don't want to."

"What don't you want?"

"I will not go back."

"What?"

For a moment they looked into each other's eyes.

"You know?" Abel asked in a whisper.

Martin nodded. Abel walked a few paces towards the mahagony desk. When he turned, there was a pistol in his hand. The safety catch gave a faint click.

Martin stood up. "But that is absurd — "

Abel slowly came up to Martin. "Here," he said, handing him the weapon. "Shoot me. You must aim at this area," he pointed to where his bullet hole had once been. "Take about three paces back and make sure your hand does not shake. I want just one good, clean shot. Count up to three, to give yourself a deadline, so that you don't hesitate."

"I shouldn't dream of it."

"Don't be silly," expostulated Abel. "You are wasting time for both of us. If you don't do it, I'll have to do it myself, but in either case you will be responsible. Well, how about it?"

"No."

"Just as you like. Now I still have to bequeath you something," Abel hurried on "What would you like?"

"Nothing," snapped Martin.

"Don't you need any furniture?" Abel pointed to the pieces in the room.

"No."

"Well, take this paperweight. I think it is onyx. And now, goodbye."

Abel put the pistol to his breast, counted up to three and pulled the trigger. The recoil threw him back into the sofa. The next moment Abel briskly jumped up and brushed his coat around the place where the shot had gone through. The fine nap of the cloth was singed there. A landscape with a range of mountains in the background could be seen through the bullet hole.

"Well, that is that," said Abel. A buzzer on the desk sounded. Abel pressed one of the buttons and the voice of a secretary came from the instrument.

"The new case from Raven Street has arrived."

"Where is he?" asked Abel curtly.

"Waiting in the reception room."

"I shall be there right away. Meanwhile, let in a few smallish clouds."

Martin reached for the paperweight, which was lying on the desk.

"Leave it alone," Abel admonished him. "Our conference is over. Excuse me.'' He gave Martin a farewell nod and disappeared through a small side door.

Martin looked around the room. ''It will be terribly hard work,'' he thought. For a moment he lost courage. He walked slowly round the room.

When he came to the glass wall, he stopped. The child in the garden had disappeared. Martin was seized with grave doubts.

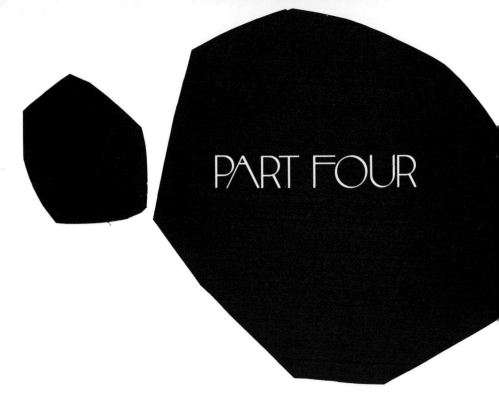

PART FOUR

14

The room was flooded with an artificial evening light. Martin tried to muster his courage. He picked up the heavy onyx paperweight from the table and played with it nervously. The buzzer went and Martin pressed the button.

"Surely you can see now that it is impossible," insisted a voice resembling Abel's.

Martin switched the loudspeaker off. His mind was made up. He crossed over to the glass wall and leaned against it with his hands. For a second he automatically braced his muscles, but he realized straight away how absurd that was. He did not expect to feel any impact, of course, but what happened surprised him all the same.

The substance of the wall instantly evaporated, as it were, and all that remained was its shape, formed of air. What should have been resistance turned into a gliding flight. The wall rushed back like a piece of scenery on wheels. Martin wanted to say something, but it was a paean of triumph that came from his throat. What he had accomplished lay beyond the bounds of simplicity. The thought flashed through his mind that he could not survive what had happened, but he was blissfully reconciled to that. He felt only an impersonal interest in how long this state of a total suspension of order could last. He approached the second wall of the room and repeated the same action; the wall moved away somewhere out of sight. The remaining two walls did not resist Martin either.

He bent down to pick up what was left of Abel's office. It was the onyx paperweight, which he must have dropped when he set out to attack the first wall. Martin picked it up and decided that he would keep it.

He looked about to enjoy his achievement, but he froze with amazement: around him towered the walls of the prison cell where he had lately been fettered to the wall. The jailer was not there, but several silver-grey clock-work mice were running about on the floor.

It took Martin a while to grasp the situation: he was not a prisoner, it was only that prison walls stood round him. What is more, they could be removed with a touch. Martin gave a sigh of relief. Then he settled himself comfortably on the floor and placed the paperweight in front of him. It looked extremely incongruous there; it introduced a different world into the cell and the confrontation suggested something ineffable. Martin followed the silent combat intently, until at last the paperweight and the prison attained equilibrium inside him. It happened quite suddenly.

"Oh-ho, oh-ho," sang Martin as he got up from the floor. He put the paperweight in his pocket and added one of the mice, which had meanwhile run down. Then, filled with tense expectation, he rapidly began to remove the walls of the jail.

This time he found himself in the underground cave, on the shore of the foul-smelling lake. There was not a soul to be seen. The boat was back in its place and the dark blue peaked cap was lying on its seat. Martin added it to his trophies and effortlessly leaned against the nearest wall. It gave way as easily as all the previous ones. Martin was now in a great hurry. Things were becoming clearer and clearer to him, but at the same time his impatience was growing.

Soon he was standing in the throne room, which was blazing with light. Martin went over to a richly decorated wall, bent down and picked up the child's ring with the little yellow stone from under the carpet. He stood lost in thought over this next property. Then with a sigh he slipped it into his pocket and attacked the walls around him.

The next place he came to was the royal baths. Here Martin found his old clothes thrown over an armchair. He quickly changed and then glanced into the hall of mirrors. His image, not entirely clear and distinct as yet, glimmered faintly in the countless mirror panes. He turned to the pool, pulled out a purple-red ball and promptly added it to his collection. He took a deep breath and approached one of the side walls of the baths.

The vast, darkened hall of astrology greeted Martin with all its stars. The deserted space looked even larger than the first time Martin entered it. The motion of the empty tables made his head spin. Martin began to whistle under his breath. He stood in the middle of the hall and watched the complicated interlocking of their motion. After a while a table with a gold paper star lying on it came towards him. Martin picked up the star and pensively put it in his pocket. It took him some time to make up his mind to attack the first wall of the hall of astrology.

He was surrounded by the walls of the testing room. All the apparatus, mechanisms, and preparations lay here in perfect order, suggesting a museum exhibition. Martin made his way to the section of psychological tests and found the table with the colored wooden blocks. Thoughtfully he piled them up into various patterns, and then a cube of vivid green struck his fancy. He added it to the other souvenirs and sat down heavily.

The next day a fishing boat carried Martin away, its motor puffing bravely over the wide plain of the sea. But none of the fishermen could remember a sailing ship ever having gone down in those waters. Then, in the bow, Martin noticed an old sack containing an axe, a piece of sail, a rope, an old sweater, a skin of drinking water, some grease-soaked rags, an iron hook, and a rusty lantern. The fishermen indignantly denied that they had found these things. Martin pacified them with a few words and asked them to give him the sack and the skin. After hesitating for a moment they did so and then watched with sullen eyes as Martin poured the drinking water out and filled the skin with sea water. They sat there, gutting and cleaning the fish they had caught, with the churlish expression of men who cannot abide waste.

Some hours later the boat landed at the stone jetty. The little port town lay spread out along the shore at the foot of the steep cliff. The local fish-canning factory was pouring ribbons of black smoke into the air. Still wobbly from the boat, Martin set out into the streets. He asked several times about the goat track but received only negative answers. The people he accosted examined him suspiciously; they had grown accustomed to the eccentricities of the foreigners who occasionally came there, but this was something new. They could not understand why anyone should want to scramble up the cliff when he could go and sit on a bus. Martin soon gave up trying and made his way to the station. After rather a long time the bus came and Martin was profoundly relieved to see the conductor.

"You did not come to any harm, then," he greeted him joyfully. "I was reproaching myself."

"I beg your pardon?"

while. The quarreling voices of the buyers and sellers came to him from afar, wafted on the monotonous melody of the strange tongue. Somewhere a radio blared. The sun was already setting in the west when Martin started on the next stage of his journey.

The impenetrably dark subterranean passage seemed to have no end. Martin was obliged to walk very slowly, often relying on his sense of touch alone. He had torn a hole near the edge of the sack so that he could put his head through it, and now he carried it round his neck. It was throttling him, but both his hands were free. He stumbled on step by step, worn out with irritation rather than fatigue. He felt that he had traversed the whole of eternity before he finally came to the dimly lit cave. He broke off a little pink-tinted stalactite there, and impatiently continued his journey. Before long he was standing in front of a heavy oak door. With a little effort he opened it and found himself in the shop of the dealer of disguises. It was empty. Then a door clicked somewhere.

"Can I help you, sir?" a voice asked at Martin's back. It was a little old man, who was slowly shuffling forward by the counter.

"What can I do for you?"

"I had some things from here," began Martin. "Where is the owner?"

"I am the owner," demurred the little old man. "You ought to sit down for a minute, sir. You look as if you were about to faint. What is that around your neck?"

"I feel great," Martin cut him short. He pulled the sack off over his head and put it on the ground.

"Your trouser-legs are all torn."

Martin discovered that the old man was not exaggerating.

"That was the passage," he tried to explain, but then he realized it was useless.

"Couldn't you lend me some disguise?"

"What do you mean by disguise? I am a bookbinder, sir. Maybe you have come to the wrong address, haven't you?" The little old man studied Martin attentively and took pity on him.

"Look, I have an apprentice here; if you like, I can send him to your apartment to get you some clothes. You can't go out into the street like this. You need not worry, sir, he is an honest boy and he will be glad to make a few extra pennies. And that luggage of yours," the old man added tactfully, "you can leave it here for the time being and come back for it tomorrow."

Martin agreed; he gave the boy his address and the old man sat him down on an old sofa. "I'll go and make some coffee. You are not a local man, are you?"

"Yes I am," replied Martin, "but I have been — traveling."

"That's it, that's it," the bookbinder nodded. "And what is it like out there? An old man like me no longer gets to go anywhere, you know. Once I used to read a lot, at least, but I don't even do that any more. I just bind the books now. You would not believe, sir, what a lot of stuff has been written over all these centuries. But nowadays I merely bind it in hard covers. I am just not interested any more. I turn all those words into things a man can put on a bookshelf. That is something, too."

"So you have not found anything in all those books?"

"Oh, I shouldn't say that. I found something. But the main things . . . " The coffee pot on the ring began to boil over and the old man ran to deal with it. Soon he came back, bringing two cups of steaming coffee.

"What you have out there in the world isn't everything either," the old man pursued his idea. "But it has to be seen. That's a fact. When I was young I saw a bit of the world, too."

Martin tasted the hot coffee. It had the good, reliable taste he knew. "Well, where then — ?" He tried to draw the old man out. The bookbinder shrugged.

"If I only knew that, I'd write it all down." He sipped his coffee and continued matter-of-factly, "Most likely in life. In those few joys a man can have. — But perhaps not even that," he added after a while. Once more he drank some coffee and then, with resignation but without repining, he finished his idea. "Maybe there actually isn't any such thing."

Martin felt a chill round his heart.

"I shall find out this evening," he said curtly. "This evening, as soon as I get home."

"Well, mind you come and tell me all about it as soon as you do" said the little old man, quite unperturbed. His head was beginning to nod. "But generally one runs around in circles — like a dog chasing its own tail."

His heart beating, Martin opened the door and walked into the room where he had lived before he started out on his travels. It seemed a little smaller, of course, but all the more expressive for that; it had even kept its rather peculiar, agreeable smell. The faint whistle of a locomotive came from the far-off station. Martin looked about. There by the window stood his iron bed with its counterpane, next to it the ramshackle wardrobe, then, in the middle, the square table with two chairs and, by the opposite wall, the washbasin, the small cupboard with the gas ring and the little heater in the corner. On the wall, instead of a picture, there hung a period map of the then known world. Everything was in its place, even the odds and ends left over from the house-cleaning were still lying by the door.

Martin bent down impatiently to this little pile and started carrying it piece by piece over to the table. First there was a black paperweight, then a silver-grey mouse with broken clockwork, a worn out blue peaked cap, a ring with a little yellow stone, a peeling red ball, a gold paper star, a green wooden block; then a handful of black soil, a crystal pebble, some salty liquid in a bottle without a label, a twig with some dried leaves, a few grains of sand, and a fragment of pinkish stick that seemed to be made of glass.

Martin sat down over these things. The twilight in the room grew denser. There, in a few tokens, the whole of his journey was spread out before him. Martin guessed that the key to the secret lay hidden somewhere here — if only he knew how to look. Once more he gazed at his collection, bored into it with an ever more piercing stare, but that did not lead anywhere. "I don't know what to do," Martin almost cried out in desperation. "I can't make it out!"

Pictures from his journey flitted through his mind, all jumbled together: the cave, the lens-polisher, the aurochs, the hall of astrology, Abel, the oasis, the executioner, the forest clearing, the ship. He shook his head frantically. There on the table the things lay, their outlines sharply distinct and their surfaces firmly closed. And there opposite them sat he, with slightly bulging eyes. He found himself ridiculous. Besides, the thickening twilight in the room was making it harder and harder to see. The things on the table were gradually losing their color, their shapes were dissolving in dark patches. Martin soon grew quite calm; he rocked back in his chair and made himself comfortable. All at once, something cheered him. He opened the table drawer and took out a sheet of paper and a pencil. It was not quite an idea yet, but already he knew the solution. "Hey, hey," he brayed joyfully to himself. And he started to write. It was slow work, much slower than he had anticipated in his excitement, but he knew he was doing the right thing. After every few words he picked up one of the objects and carried it back to the door. The dusk was fast growing blacker, so he was obliged to write from memory. He did his best to make big, clear letters, which would be easy to read in the light. When he finished, the things he had brought to the table were back in a pile by the door and the sheet of paper was covered with a list on which they were all entered. But it was not just an inventory, for it gave each thing its proper name. The catalogue Martin had drawn up looked like this.

Stalactite from the cave of disguises and masks
Sand from the oasis of blood
Twig from the desert of ghosts
Water from the wandering ship
Pebble from the house of the corrector of vision
Soil from the forest of life

These names formed the first group. The next paragraph contained the following.

Green block of the regulators
Gold star of the fortune-tellers
Purple ball of the servants of the elect
Yellow ring of the empress-infanta
Blue cap of Hades
Grey mouse of the guardians of the underworld

Finally, quite apart from the rest, stood the last name.

Paperweight from angelic space

Martin hummed contentedly to himself as he went over and over his catalogue. Now and then he rewrote or added a word, tightened up an expression here, altered one there, sometimes he changed the original name altogether. Again and again he thought he had found the final wording and again and again he went back and made corrections. It was long after midnight when he adopted one of the versions as final. But it was not final, it was only the last one.

Once more, rather mechanically this time, he went over the names he had discovered. Only a moment ago they had seemed perfect, and now to his horror he found that their content was evaporating; slowly but inexorably the names were deflating and turning into mere words. Martin tried to keep them alive by forcibly altering their wording, but he already knew the battle was lost. He stared at the sheet of paper covered with writing and then at the pile of things by the door.

"The whole thing is utterly unreal," he mumbled helplessly. His chin dropped with weariness. For a moment he lost consciousness. Suddenly, a streak of lightning flashed through his head and his limbs jerked violently, as if they had received a shock. He was awake. As if guided by a helping power, he seized the list of names, struck a match and set light to it. The fire eagerly devoured the paper and turned it to ash. Martin got up. He looked at his lodging and at once, for the first time since he had been living there, he saw it; he absorbed it into himself in an infallible experience. It was his home.

He looked at the things piled at the door and they seemed to him like the discarded outer shell of some living creature; in one broad, penetrating survey he took this life into himself in its integrity. It was his life.

He went to the window and opened it; it was beginning to grow light. Martin raised his eyes and saw the sky; it permeated him with its fresh light and he saw the break of day. It was the dawn of the world.

He felt himself gaining in strength, lucidity, wholeness. He felt the unsuspected expanse of reality surging up within him.

In the fountain in the square, water was gushing in several streams. Martin called up within himself the song this water sang, in order to capture it; after a while he actually began to hum the song quietly to himself; and now it was living water . . . .